Saving His Soulmate

Ruth Madison

*10% of net royalties from the sale of the Sledge Hockey Team Of Cedar Harbor series will be **donated to https://www.bostonicestorm.org/** Boston's only sled hockey team founded and managed by people with disabilities.*

Titles In The Series

Thawing An Ice Heart

Saving His Soulmate

Hearts Unmasked

Love Comes Back

Holiday Stories

Contents

Cedar Harbor   VI

Map   VII

      VIII

1. Samantha   1

2. Robbie   7

3. Samantha   21

4. Robbie   32

5. Samantha   48

6. Robbie   54

7. Samantha   71

8. Robbie   79

9. Samantha   94

10. Robbie   100

11. Samantha   106

12. Robbie   113

13. Samantha   127

14. Robbie   132

15. Samantha   141

16. Robbie   148

17. Becca   155

Other Books By Ruth Madison

<u>The Unbroken Novella Series (</u>_Kindle Unlimited)_

The Billionaire's Secretary

Wheely Into You

<u>Stand Alone And Other</u>

The World Between Us

Waiting To Break

<u>Sled Hockey Team Of Cedar Harbor Series</u>

Thawing An Ice Heart

Saving His Soulmate

Hearts Unmasked

Love Comes Back

Get Bonus Content For All Books At:

ruthmadisonbooks.com/bonus

Samantha

What people don't realize about working in a grocery store is that it's like a family. It's not just knowing that the guy at the deli counter has a crush on the lady in bakery or that the evening security guard will be your best friend if you bring her a scratch-off ticket. It's the customers too. I work the register and sometimes monitor the self-check machines. There are people who always find my line to check out and we chat while I ring up their groceries. And at the self-check I love to entertain the babies and kids so their parents can focus on checking out. I try to make every person I encounter smile and I've got a pretty good average. There's always new people but there's also always plenty of familiar faces.

Like Robbie.

I don't know what it is about him but when I see him roll into the store my whole mood lifts. If it isn't too busy my manager lets me go and help him. He's the kind of guy who you can tell is tall and lanky even though he can't stand up.

"Hey, Robbie," I say walking up to him.

I don't even have to try to get him to smile, his whole face lights up when he sees me. He's wearing sneakers and long basketball shorts with a shopping basket balanced on his lap. He leans back a bit and slides his sunglasses to the top of his head with the side of one hand.

"Hi, Sam."

He told me once that people assume he's paraplegic because he can use a manual wheelchair and move his arms but he's actually a quadriplegic because his hands have some paralysis too. His legs are long and I can see his bare calves quivering a tiny bit.

"How was hockey practice?"

"So much fun. I think we're going to have our first game against another team soon. Just need a couple more players."

"How cool! I hope I can come and watch. Let me know when it is."

"Of course," he says. "We need all the cheerleaders we can get."

I look at his list. "What is this weird assortment of things?"

"My sister cooks for me a lot, I don't usually need much in terms of ingredients."

"I can't believe you like the hot chili flavor chips." I shake my head in mock disappointment as I slide my finger down the paper.

"Why? Which flavor do you like?" he says.

"The correct answer is cheddar and sour cream."

"If it doesn't burn going down, it's not worth it." He grins his cheeky grin at me and I laugh.

We walk around the store together and I reach things from high shelves for him. Without full use of his hands, gripping things is challenging too so sometimes I put the things in the basket while he just pushes his chair. Robbie uses the sides of his hands on the pushrims of his wheelchair. There's a groove between his thumbs and first fingers that can almost get a grip on the metal rims.

"I need your expert opinion," he says, "which of these peanut butters should I get?"

Working as a cashier does not in fact make me an expert on any kind of food. If I worked in one of the departments that might be a different story. I am an expert on where to find obscure ingredients, when the newest deliveries of milk come in, and things like that. I often wander the store and talk to the people in every department so I know what's going on both in gossip and in stocking.

But Robbie is just kidding and I play along. Together we consider the different peanut butter choices.

"Do you prefer creamy or crunchy?" he asks.

"Crunchy," I say without hesitation. "What about you?"

"Agreed," he says.

After a few more aisles he asks, "Did you finish the book I got you?"

"I did!" Last time I saw him Robbie gave me a copy of Treasure Island. He said it was his childhood favorite and he was shocked I had never read it.

"What did you think?"

"Loved it," I say honestly. "I thought it would be more clear good guy v.s. bad guy but there's a lot of gray morality, which is fascinating. I've got a book for you this time. Remind me when we get to the register." Growing up I was very limited in what I was allowed to read or watch. I'm not surprised Treasure Island was out because there's nothing my parents hate more than the concept of gray morality.

We pass by the fish and I wave at my friend behind the counter. Inside the store is kind of like a little village where everyone knows everyone else. It's a complete world to itself. When we reach the chip aisle it is almost entirely blocked by a third party vendor restocking the shelves. When he sees Robbie's wheelchair he turns red as a beet and scrambles to push all his boxes to the side. I thank him as we pass single file.

It doesn't take long to get everything on Robbie's eclectic little list and I'm sad that our time together is coming to an end. It's stupid that I'm feeling this way. I'm married. I shouldn't be feeling anything more than plain friendship for Robbie. But I cherish the time we spend together and I never want it to end. And in secret I have to admit there's just something about Robbie's shaggy brown hair and big doe eyes that makes my heart flutter.

As I'm packing up his groceries, I slip a copy of The Hobbit into his bag. "If you like adventures, you're going to love this one," I say.

"See you next time," he says.

"Let me help you out," Tom says, appearing as though out of nowhere. He sometimes bags but usually he's bringing carts back from the parking lot and charging scooters. He carries Robbie's bags to his car for him.

My shift is coming to an end and I try to ignore the tightening in my gut.

Of course I want to go home and spend the evening with my husband. I just hope that he's had a good day. My husband is a sweet guy but he's often misunderstood and he gets frustrated. He has a hard time holding down a job and it makes things tense sometimes because it's not easy to live on a grocery store salary in eastern Massachusetts. But we manage.

I never know what kind of mood he'll be in when I get home but I buy an ice cream sandwich before leaving the store so I can cheer him up if he's down.

Robbie

I wheel out of the grocery store with a small cardboard box of food on my lap. It's easier to balance than a bag. I appreciate about Cedar Harbor that it's such a small town everything is walking distance. At least it is for me as someone who runs three miles every morning (in a racing-style wheelchair, of course). Once snow is on the ground it will get a lot harder for me to get around but the town is good about shoveling the sidewalks so it's not too bad.

I'm moving slowly because there's always a risk of hitting a bump and the box of groceries falling off my lap. Then I'm shit out of luck. With more than half my body paralyzed, I can't do anything about it if I spill a bunch of stuff. But the few times it has happened I've always been able to flag someone down to help.

As I head towards my apartment I wonder what book I should bring Sam next. I love to see how her face lights up when I present her with a new one. No one thinks that I'm a reader. That's stereotypes for you. Just because I am involved in four different sports and run every morning doesn't mean I don't also appreciate great books.

I don't have an excuse to go to the grocery store all that often since my sister loves to cook and lives in the same building as me and we often have dinner together. But I look forward to my trips just to see Sam. She's a good friend. We love to talk and I always feel happy around her. I know she's married, I'm not trying to mess with her like that. I just enjoy her company, that's all.

My wheels crunch over drifts of crisp dry leaves that have blown across the sidewalks. I've never minded the cold and now I have even more reason to enjoy it because of my new obsession, the sled hockey team my sister's boyfriend has started.

I'm glad Carly finally found someone. She works so hard for other people, she deserves someone to care for her too. Tonight will be dinner at her place and though it used to be just she and I, now Murph is always there too. I don't mind the extra company. Murph and I have a lot in common since we both love sports and we're both wheelchair users. To be honest, some nights Carly gets left out of the conversation completely if he and I get going about baseball or football.

Outside my apartment door I pull up my keycard. The apartment complex owners have been super understanding about disability issues and instead of a regular key I just need to touch the card to the door to open it. It's still a little tricky to push open the door and not drop my box of groceries. As I'm working at it my neighbor, Betty, appears heading for the elevator. She's wearing a puffy vest and carrying a single ski pole like a walking stick.

"Afternoon, Rob, how are you today?" she asks brightly.

"Doing great," I say with a grin.

"Let me hold that door for you, dear."

"Thank you much!" I gladly roll back for her to open my door for me.

Once I'm inside, Betty says, "I'm off for my constitutional, see you later."

I put away my few things. Mostly just snacks and Gatorade. It's just about time for my work shift so I take one bottle of the sports drink and a package of Hostess cupcakes and head for my desk.

I slip the headset over my ears and test the mic. "Shipping Solutions, this is Rob," I say to the empty room, checking that my voice doesn't echo too much before the real calls start.

By 1:00 pm on the dot, the first line flashes. "Yes, ma'am," I tell a breathless voice on the other end, "if you read me that tracking number one more time, I'll find it." She does, haltingly, and I type it in with two knuckles, the cursor blinking like it's impatient. "Looks like your sweater set's in Des Moines. Weather delay. I'll keep an eye on it."

She thanks me three times, voice soft with relief. When the call ends, I grin to myself. If she could see me right now...young guy in a manual wheelchair, wearing a hoodie, Gatorade balanced between my thighs. She'd never guess. There's something quietly funny about that. Whole world calling me for help, and not one of them knows I'm paralyzed.

Entertainment comes in small doses. You take what you can get.

Another call buzzes through. Billing issue. I navigate the software, tap the mute button with the side of my hand when I need to cough. By the time I hang up, my silent alarm is already buzzing against my thigh. Time to shift.

I press my fists against the cushion and lift just enough to ease the pressure from my hips. I can't feel it but I've had years of practice gauging exactly how much to push up. One, two, three. Lower back down. The faint hiss of the air cushion settles under me again. That little dance every half hour keeps my skin intact. Miss a few, and you're playing with fire.

I learned that the hard way at nineteen. Thought I was invincible and ended up in the hospital staring at the same ceiling tile for seven days, dreaming about basketball drills I couldn't do. Lesson learned. Now I treat my skin right.

The next four hours blur into clicks, voices, and the rhythm of small shifts. When my work timer chimes, I stretch my neck until it pops, peel off the headset, and roll backward with a long exhale.

Shower time.

I wheel into the bathroom and glance at the clock. Before my accident, I used to brag about five-minute showers. These days, forty-five feels like a win.

The process starts with patience. Jacket off. Shirt over my head. Each sleeve tugged free with a fist hooked through the fabric. Then pants: lean, tug, adjust, swear once under my breath when the denim catches on my ankle.

The transfer to the shower chair takes focus. Hands lock on the rails, arms tense, body slides. I turn on the water and it hits the tile with a sharp hiss, filling the air with steam and the clean smell of soap. I lean forward, feeling droplets run down the back of my neck and then the sensation disappears.

The next part's easy—lather, rinse, let the heat sink in. It's what comes after that sucks. I drape a towel across my wheelchair seat before I transfer back, because wet cushions and bare skin are a bad mix. Then the drying, the dressing, the tug and pull and settle of each layer.

By the time I'm done, the bathroom mirror's fogged over and the clock's inched past forty minutes. Just in time to head out to Carly's apartment for dinner. My hair is still a bit damp but it's short and will air dry quickly. I take the elevator down two floors and knock on Carly's door.

As always she yells for me to just come in. I work the handle with the side of my fist and push my way inside.

Her boyfriend, Kevin Murphy, is already there. Almost everyone calls him "Murph" except my sister. She's the only one I know who calls him "Kevin." He's pouring the wine while Carly finishes the food. Her small kitchen table is getting a little crowded with three of us but she didn't have to get a second chair since Murph and I both bring our own everywhere we go.

Our disabilities aren't the same, though. While I'm paralyzed from about my nipples down, Murph is an amputee. He lost both his legs to an IED many years ago. I learned that from my sister. Murph never talks about his time in battle. Even though he could walk with prosthetics, he rarely does. He says the wheelchair is just easier.

So he can feel what body he has left and I can only feel a small percentage of mine. Spinal cord injuries are always unique and there's almost never a clear line of demarcation between sensation and not. Like I can't feel my legs, torso, or hands at all, but I can feel my right forearm and my left upper arm. Then from about nipples up, I'm good. We've had to adapt some of the sled hockey equipment for my hands' lack of grip but Murph always finds a way to make it work.

"Hey, man, good to see you," I say as I join him. We actually already saw each other at hockey practice this morning but whatever.

"Feeling sore from practice at all?" he asks.

"Just a little," I admit. Pushing the hockey sled does utilize different muscles from my other sports. My body will catch up soon, I have no doubt.

Murph isn't a big talker and with baseball season wrapped up for the year, we're a little sparse on topics.

"What's on the menu tonight?" I ask.

Of course, Carly has cooked an incredible gourmet meal as though it's no big deal. From the stove she practically sings her answer, "Seared salmon, salad, and garlic chive mashed potatoes with fruit tart for dessert."

I am so spoiled.

Minutes later we've all got our plates and I'm getting creative with my knife and fork since my fingers don't work anymore. It's silent except for the occasional moan of pleasure while we chow down. Carly is a magician in the kitchen. She cooks a lot of the things that our grandmother used to make us but secretly I think Carly does it better.

Throughout dinner I can't help noticing that Carly and Murph keep giving each other little looks and smiles. Of course they're dating so it makes sense but it's not really their style. I feel like there's some kind of secret or joke that I'm left out of.

Finally I say, "Is there something you want to tell me?"

Carly smiles and nods. She grasps Murph's hand and says, "We do have some news."

What is she going to tell me? There's no way they're engaged already although I'm certain they are meant for each other.

"Kevin and I are going to move in together," Carly says. Then she rushes out the speech she's probably been practicing all day, "We're buying a condo on the other side of town. I just want to reassure you that we'll still be close by and our dinners don't have to change at all."

"That's awesome. Congratulations you two." It really is great news. I have watched my sister bury herself in work for years and it's a relief that she's found someone to be her partner and to even out her perfectionistic tendencies.

After we finish eating, Carly washes and I dry. It's our unspoken rhythm now—her sleeves rolled up, me balancing plates on my lap and towel-drying them before passing them to the counter. Murph hasn't quite found his place in the system yet, so he hangs back, elbows resting on the edge of the table, a quiet grin tugging at his mouth.

"Since it's almost Thanksgiving," Carly says, "I think Mom and Dad are going to come up to help with the move." She wipes the back of her wrist across her forehead, leaving a stripe of suds tangled in her hair. I grin but don't mention it yet.

I look over at Murph. "Meeting the parents, huh?" My tone is light, but the weight of it's there. For all our talk about moving boxes and lease paperwork, this is the real milestone.

He nods. "Yep. Can't decide—legs or no legs?"

The dish in my hands drips onto my jeans while I think about it. That's not a flippant question. I know exactly what he means. He could wear the prosthetics, look more "whole" for their first impression. Our parents already know he's an amputee, but seeing it is different. Maybe it'd make them feel more comfortable about Carly's future, make them see him as "capable." I know better than anyone how unintentionally ableist they are. On the other hand, he hasn't worn the legs once since I met him.

If he shows up in prosthetics, he's setting a version of himself he doesn't actually live. But if he doesn't...well, I know my mom. She'll paste on a smile and then go home to "process her feelings" for a week.

Murph chuckles when he sees my face twisting through all that mental math. "Didn't mean to short-circuit your brain, man. Give it some thought and get back to me."

Carly flicks a bit of soap at him. "You're not a science experiment, Kev."

He grins. "Feels like it sometimes."

I set the damp plate on the rack and finally notice that I've made my lap soaking wet. "Okay," I say at last. "Here's my vote: no legs. Meet them exactly how you live. Better to let them see what everyday looks like than put on a show for a weekend."

Carly's drying her hands now, watching me. "You think they won't freak out?"

"Oh, they'll freak out," I say. "Just in a polite, New England, 'pass the stuffing' kind of way. But they'll get over it. You don't need to ease them in, you just need to give them something solid to hold onto. Show them that you two are happy, that you've got life handled. That'll calm them faster than any pair of fancy legs."

Murph taps the wheel rim with his knuckles, thoughtful. "That makes sense. Are they likely to ask a lot of invasive questions?"

"Yes," Carly mutters emphatically.

"I'll be the bad cop if needed," I say. "If they wander into medical territory or 'but have you tried...,' I'll steer it. And if they need reassurance about safety or the move, we anchor it to specifics: budget, chore split, your schedule, rides for appointments...grown-up stuff. Trust me, I've been through this with our parents more times than I can count. Carly, when you Facetime mom you can lay out a clear plan for exactly when the Thanksgiving meal is, and when packing and unpacking is. Give them the parameters so you have some breathing room."

Carly exhales, a shaky smile starting. "I can do that."

I grin and finally point at the soap bubbles in her hair. "You might wanna wipe your head before you make the call, though. Kind of ruins your credibility."

She laughs and smacks my arm with the dish towel.

Murph's smile softens. "Thanks, man. Appreciate it."

"Anytime," I say. "You're family now. Besides, if they give you a hard time, I'll roll over their toes."

Carly leans over to wrap an arm around each of us, squeezing our shoulders. "Team," she says.

"Team," Murph and I answer together.

When I get back to my apartment, the door clicks shut behind me with that soft hollow sound I always notice more on nights like this. The kind of sound that reminds you you're alone. My wheels hum against the hardwood as I roll toward the center of the space and stop, staring at nothing for a few seconds. The quiet feels thick after being at Carly's. Her place always buzzes with motion: her voice, the sound of pans clattering, Murph's laugh rumbling low. Here, it's just the faint hum of the heater and the ticking of the kitchen clock.

I let out a long breath and tilt my head back. God, I'm tired. The evening was good. Comfortable. But change has a way of finding the cracks, even in something good.

I glance toward the counter where Carly always sets the groceries when she comes over after her workday. The space looks bare without her canvas bag sitting there. She's been my anchor these last few years: my emergency contact, my backup plan, my family right down the road. And now, everything's shifting.

I wheel into the kitchen, the faint scent of dish soap still clinging to my sleeves from earlier. My hands ache a little from overuse; I flex them carefully. She deserves this. Murph's good for her, steady, solid in a way she needs. They fit together so well it's hard not to feel proud watching it.

Still, there's a small, selfish part of me that wants to hit pause. Just keep things how they've been: her close, our routines intact. I've built a good life here but there's comfort in knowing my sister is five minutes away if something goes sideways. I tell myself I don't rely on that...but the truth is, I do. In the back of my mind, I always know she's there. It's not like she's moving to Antartica. She'll be on the other side of town and it's not even a big town.

My eyes drift to the corner of the table where my phone sits charging. For a moment, I picture it lighting up and Sam's name glowing across the screen.

Of course, it doesn't.

I can see her in my mind anyway: behind the grocery store register, smiling at customers, hair tucked behind one ear. The way she always remembers what kind of cereal I buy. The way her voice softens when she says my name.

I shake my head, trying to clear it. "Don't go there," I mutter to myself.

She's married. She's off-limits.

But the image lingers and something inside me aches, even as I try to ignore it.

I wheel back toward the bedroom. Shadows stretch across the floor like water. My body's heavy, but my mind keeps humming: half in the past, half in a future I can't quite see yet.

As I transfer into bed, the quiet folds in again, wrapping tight around the edges of the night. Carly's moving forward. Maybe it's time I find a way to do the same.

Still, as I stare up at the ceiling, against my better judgment, Sam's face is the last thing I see before sleep finally drags me under.

Samantha

I come home with my peace offering, but Will isn't impressed. He's slouched in front of the TV, eyes fixed on the screen, not even glancing up when I walk in.

"I brought you an ice cream sandwich from work," I say.

He finally looks over, a sneer spreading across his face. "Ice cream? What is wrong with you, woman? How are you this stupid?"

"It's fine," I say quickly. "It hasn't melted." I hold it out, but he takes it only to toss it straight into the trash can. It lands with a soft thud. It really hadn't melted.

I swallow my words. It's not worth another fight. "I'll get started on dinner," I whisper.

Our house sits right on the edge of the woods. Out the kitchen window, bare branches tangle together like bony fingers, almost blocking out the pale, icy sky. As I sprinkle salt over the pork chops, the sizzle of the pan fills the silence. Will calls himself a *meat and potatoes guy*, which means my cooking can never be too creative. No spices, no sauces; just salt, pepper, and grease. Comfort food for a man who refuses comfort.

While the pork chops brown, I pour powdered mashed potatoes into a pot and watch the flakes dissolve into paste. He's the only person I know who prefers boxes potatoes.

Will's had a hard life. When we first met, I thought love could fix that. I believed if I was patient enough, gentle enough, steady enough, I could heal him. I still want to believe that. But every day it feels like I'm pouring water into a cracked glass—no matter how much I give, it's never full.

Sometimes it feels like I wake up every morning with a new plan for how to reach him. A softer tone, a longer hug, a special dinner. None of it lasts. I didn't know, when we married, that love could turn into walking on eggshells. No one would *choose* this, not consciously. But my upbringing didn't teach me to recognize healthy relationships.

When we met, Will was charming. Funny, attentive, always talking about dreams he never intended to chase.

He said he had a job, but it turned out he mostly fishes and lives off the rent from his mother's Cape house. I should have left when I learned that. But I didn't.

I don't tell many people the truth: I grew up in a cult. I ran away when I was seventeen, but running doesn't erase everything you've been taught. I came out of it with no family, no life skills, and this deep, unshakable belief that my purpose was to listen, to soothe, to make men's lives easier.

Old habits die hard.

I was too quick to try to find a man to latch onto. I'm mad at myself for that but I have empathy for the girl I used to be. She didn't know any other way. Even though she figured out the cult wasn't leading her where she wanted to go, the only way she knew to make sense of life was to find a man to take care of.

By the time of my wedding I probably would have told you that I left the people who taught me that a woman's only purpose in life is to be a selfless and perfect wife but I couldn't see that somewhere deep inside I still believed it.

Cooking gives me too much time to think, so I grab my purse and pull out the book Robbie lent me. I set it on the counter, trying to read between stirring potatoes and turning the pork chops. I only half succeed.

By the time dinner's on the table, the meat's a little black around the edges. Will glares at his plate. "You are so dumb," he mutters. "It's a miracle I put up with you."

I say nothing. Last time I argued, he held my wrist against the hot stove until my skin blistered. Silence is safer. But silence angers him too. He grabs my chin and jerks my face toward his. His fingers dig into my cheeks.

"Don't you agree?" he demands.

"Yes," I say softly. "I'm sorry you have to put up with my stupidity."

He doesn't catch the edge of exhaustion in my voice, just nods, satisfied. "You're lucky to have me," he mutters, eyes on his plate. "You wouldn't survive a week on your own."

Maybe he's right. Growing up, I learned rules, not life. How to obey, not how to live. I wasn't surviving very well when he met me and for a little while it really did feel like a fairytale, like a handsome prince had come to rescue me. I thought that was my reward for being brave enough to leave my family.

I assumed then that life was simple. The cult may have had the wrong answer, but there was a worldview that had the right answer and I just had to get away from the wrong one to get to the right one. Years too late I can see that's not at all how life works.

That night, I put on a nice set of matching silky pajamas even though it's not necessary. I climb into bed and brush my hand over Will's chest. He turns to me, eyes burning with lust. The only time he touches me is when he wants sex. I let him. It's the one time I feel wanted and sometimes it's enough to make me believe this is all as it should be. I'm starved for human touch most of the day, but this I can count on.

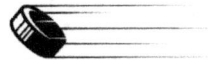

I'm relieved to have work the next morning. I'd work seven days a week if Tina let me. Stepping outside feels like shedding a heavy coat I never meant to put on. The air bites my cheeks, sharp with cold. I zip my jacket up to my chin, hands buried deep in my pockets as I trudge to the car. Frost webs across the windshield like lace.

"Damn it," I mutter. I forgot to come out early to scrape. My fingers crack and sting as I chip away at the ice. You'd never guess I've lived in New England my whole life.

When I finally get the car started, I blast the defroster and rub warmth into my hands. The dashboard clock tells me I'm already cutting it close. I'll have to hustle if I want to clock in before the grace period ends.

At the Stop N Shop, I clock in, throw my jacket into the breakroom, and head for the customer service desk. Tina assigns me to a register. Early shifts are quiet: just the night-shift workers grabbing dinner ingredients and retirees who like to start their day before sunrise.

A familiar face appears at the door. Becca. She knows my schedule better than I do.

She's my best friend. Quirky, brilliant, unapologetically herself. She used to come over to my place after work, but Will found her "annoying," and every visit ended in a fight. Now she visits me here instead.

While I ring up groceries, she stands at the end of my lane, bagging for customers. Tina pretends not to notice. Technically Becca's not supposed to be here, but she insists she's providing "free labor." Honestly, she's the best bagger I've ever had—precise and methodical, like she's solving a puzzle with every bag.

Becca's autistic, diagnosed young, which makes her something of an anomaly. We met at a Jewish summer camp when we were seven. My cult leaders approved because they thought it "taught modesty." I still don't know why the camp allowed us, but that's childhood for you—you accept the strange as normal because you don't have any context to know how odd something is.

Most girls ignored Becca, but I didn't. I liked her quiet brilliance, her odd little observations about people. She made sense to me.

These days, she has a self-improvement list, things she wants to "get better" at. I don't think she needs to fix anything, but it makes her happy, so I help. Today's goal is *small talk*.

"That's a big one," I say, grinning. "Ironically."

Becca scribbles in her notebook. "I'm writing that down."

I laugh. Her favorite thing in the world is jokes, which is just indescribably adorable. "Okay, let's start by breaking it into steps."

She frowns. "I don't know how. I don't understand it well enough to break it down."

"I'll help," I say. "I had lessons in how to make conversation growing up. Turns out The Foundation was really into teaching women to manage everyone else's emotions."

Before she can answer, a customer starts unloading groceries. Becca takes their reusable bags (Cedar Harbor banned plastic a few years ago) and gets to work.

This customer isn't one of my regulars. I see it as a challenge: how much can I brighten her morning in the few minutes we have? It's my favorite game.

"Good morning," I say. "How's your day going so far?"

She doesn't respond at first, too busy digging in her purse. I keep scanning, unfazed. "I swear, purses are like black holes," I joke. "No matter how small mine is, I can never find what I'm looking for."

She looks up and smiles. "That's the truth."

I smile back, hand her receipt, and wish her a good day.

When she leaves, I turn to Becca. "Small talk isn't really about the *words*. It's about connection. Do you know why people do it?"

She tilts her head. "To...avoid silence?"

"Partly," I say. "But mostly it's about comfort. It's a way to say *I see you*, even when you're just chatting about the weather. It makes people feel safe."

Her brows knit. "So, talk that isn't about the content."

"Exactly. Words can carry emotion even when they don't carry meaning and that can be just as important sometimes."

She nods slowly and writes again in her notebook.

Then Robbie's sister, Carly, shows up, as she does almost every shift. She shops often, always for one bag's worth of fresh food.

"Fresh fish today?" I ask, spotting the packaging.

"Couldn't resist," Carly says, grinning. "Hi, Becca!"

Becca waves without looking up.

"Dinner for one?" I ask.

"Kevin's coming over. He's been over every night this week," she says, a little blush rising in her cheeks. "No Robbie tonight, basketball practice."

I smile. "That boy and his sports."

Carly laughs. Nothing more needs to be said, we both know her brother would do every sport ever invented if there were enough hours in the day.

When she's gone, I nudge Becca. "Want to try the next customer yourself?"

Her lips press tight. That's her nervous face. "Okay," she says, voice small. She doesn't even realize how brave she is. She agreed to try even though she's almost shaking with fear. I need to remind her not to push herself too hard. I don't even know what the purpose of all this so-called self-improvement is.

A man steps up with a few items. Becca takes a deep breath. "How are you?" she asks.

"I'm right as rain," he says. "How are you?"

Her eyes go wide. Panic rising. I jump in. "She's doing great! Practicing her conversation skills. Got any tips?"

He grins. "You can't go wrong talking about the Sox."

"Good to know," I say, and he leaves chuckling.

When he's gone, I say, "See? You survived."

"That was horrendous," she says flatly.

"It's okay not to do this," I say, looking at her seriously. Her eyes dart away. "Improving yourself is great but remember to take your time with it. What happens when you push too hard and too fast?"

"I have a meltdown," she whispers.

"I'm not criticizing," I remind her. "I want you to take care of yourself, okay?"

Finally she smiles. "Okay."

"See you tomorrow?"

She nods and heads out.

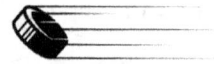

By the end of my shift, my shoulders ache but I don't want to go home. I linger, wiping down the conveyor belt, pretending there's more to do. Eventually, though, I can't delay it any longer.

No ice cream today. Maybe something else? No, he'll find a reason to mock it. I decide to go home empty-handed.

The moment I step through the door, Will barks, "You didn't bring me anything? You're such a selfish cow. Always thinking of yourself."

Explaining never helps. I stay silent, setting my purse down carefully.

"Why are you just standing there looking dumb?"

I slip into the kitchen and start dinner.

That night, I put on my prettiest underwear—the set he once called *acceptable*—and crawl into bed beside him. I reach out, searching for warmth, for touch, for anything that feels like love.

He turns to me, eyes dark with desire.

This is the rhythm of my life: work, keep Will calm, take what little tenderness I can get. It isn't great. But it's not the worst thing, either. At least, that's what I tell myself.

Robbie

Basketball was the first sport I picked up after my injury, and it stuck. No surprise: it's the gateway drug of wheelchair sports. Fast, physical, loud. For me, it still feels like freedom.

Every Thursday after work I load my basketball chair into the back of the truck and head to Thatcher Memorial. Getting in and out of the truck is its own workout. I hook my right wrist on the door handle, swing my torso up, shift my weight, and half-slide, half-muscle my way into position. Without finger grip, everything's about leverage and momentum. I've got a good system down (if you don't count the occasional curse word when the seatbelt gets tangled under me).

When I roll into the gym, the air hits me with that familiar smell of rubber, sweat, and faint lemon cleaner. The sound of wheels squealing against the glossy floor echoes off the high ceilings. The rest of the guys are already here, some stretching, some leaning back in their chairs talking trash.

"Hey, guys!" I call and heads turn.

"Hey, Robbie!" Darius shouts from across the court, spinning his chair in a full circle just to show off.

We meet near center court, exchanging high-fives and fist-bumps. The clack of metal rims bumping together is a kind of greeting music by now.

My basketball chair is different from my everyday setup. The wheels are cambered in at an angle, giving it that sleek, wide-base stance. A guard bar runs across the front, perfect for blocking—or ramming, if you ask some of the newer guys. My cushion's molded to my hips from years of use, the frame scratched from a hundred falls and just as many recoveries.

"Okay," I say, clapping my hands together out of habit—no sound, just the motion. "We're up against Watertown next week. They're strong on defense, and we all know their point guard pushes the line on steals. Can't count on the ref calling it, so tonight we're working on evasions."

The team nods. They know the drill. I'm the coach these days just based on seniority.

"Let's go two-on-two," I call. "Quick passes. Stay tight, keep your elbows clear."

The whistle echoes and the court comes alive. Wheels screech, rubber burns against the polished floor, someone yells "I'm open!" and a basketball arcs across the air. It's chaos and choreography at once—chairs darting and spinning, bumpers clanging, bodies twisting to guard the ball.

I push hard across the paint, shoulders straining, tires humming against the floor. Sweat slides down the side of my face. The ball sails towards me and I catch it between my wrists, roll back to dodge a defender while dribbling, and sling it toward Darius with a flick of my forearm. It hits his palm clean. He pivots, shoots, scores. The ball swishes through the net, that perfect sound—crisp, final, satisfying.

That's the rhythm I love. The world shrinks down to noise and motion, nothing but bodies and wheels and the sound of breath. For those moments, I'm not thinking about spinal cord injuries or pressure sores or all the things I can't do. I'm thinking about strategy, speed, and angles.

But tonight, focus keeps slipping away.

Every time we stop for water, my mind drifts back to Sam.

Last time I saw her at the grocery store she was scanning items for an elderly customer, smiling like nothing in the world was wrong, except there was that bruise on her arm. Yellow-green around the edges, new enough to stand out. Not the first time, either.

I pass the ball to Kyle and hang back a second, pretending to adjust my legs. The echo of the gym fades to a low hum as the thought needles at me again.

I want to ask her. Just straight-up ask. But what would I say? "Hey, the guy you married—does he hurt you?" You don't drop a question like that between the bread aisle and the lottery tickets.

Still, the image won't leave me: her sleeve slipping up, that quick way she tugged it back down when she caught me looking.

"Robbie!" someone calls.

I blink and wheel back into motion, catching a pass just before it flies past me. I push hard, pivot, and take the shot. The ball bounces off the rim.

"Off night, Coach!" Darius teases.

"Just giving you a confidence boost," I call back, trying to laugh it off.

We keep going. Chairs collide. Someone flips, swears, rights themselves. We play until the clock hits eight and everyone's dripping with sweat.

As we wrap up, I lean back in my chair, breathing hard. The guys are laughing, razzing each other, but my head's still somewhere else.

I hope it's nothing. God, I *want* it to be nothing.

But I've learned to trust my instincts. And the bruise wasn't nothing.

When practice wraps, the air in the gym is thick with the smell of sweat and rubber. The kind of smell that clings to your clothes and somehow feels like accomplishment.

"Good work tonight," I call as the guys start peeling away toward the locker rooms. The clatter of metal rims echoes against the walls. Someone tosses a half-empty water bottle that hits the back of my chair. I catch it on my lap and flip it upside down in mock warning.

"Careful," I say. "I'll run you over. I've got more torque than you think."

"Sure you do, old man," Kyle calls. He's twenty-one and thinks that makes him immortal.

I let the chirping roll off. They're good guys: rehab grads, vets, students, a couple who drive over from the next town just for the workout. Every one of us carries a different story about the day everything changed, but out here we're just players. No one's a diagnosis.

I roll toward the doors, the click of my casters echoing. The cold night air hits my face, sharp and welcome.

The parking lot lights throw long silver streaks across the asphalt. My truck's waiting near the curb, familiar and dented and mine.

Loading up takes time. I pop the wheels off my basketball chair one by one, lift the frame up with both wrists hooked under the crossbar, and maneuver it into the back seat. My arms tremble by the end of it, but the muscle memory carries me through. I haul myself into the driver's seat. The steering knob feels smooth under the palm of my right hand. I rest my left forearm against the mounted control and start the engine.

It's late. I should head home, get some protein, maybe stretch. But instead I find myself turning right instead of left.

The road into town glows with shop signs and holiday lights strung between lampposts. I tell myself I'm just driving to unwind after practice, that I'm not thinking about who's working the closing shift at the Stop N Shop.

But I know better.

When I pull into the grocery store parking lot, it's nearly empty, just a few cars scattered under the fluorescent lights. I sit there for a minute, engine idling, feeling stupid.

What am I going to do, roll in and pretend I suddenly need milk at nine-thirty at night? Maybe I *do* need milk. Or something.

I laugh under my breath, shake my head, and kill the engine.

Inside, the place smells like lemon cleaner and over-ripe bananas. The music's soft and forgettable. I push down the main aisle, nodding to the night stockers.

When I turn the corner near produce, I spot her. Sam's at her register, head bent, scanning a row of canned goods for the one old guy who's always here this late. Her sleeve's rolled up just enough that I can see the bruise again, darker now, almost gone yellow at the edges.

Something cold settles in my stomach.

She looks up, catches sight of me, and her face lights up. "Hey, Robbie!" she says, and that smile—damn, it still gets me.

"Hey yourself," I say easily, rolling closer. "Didn't expect to see you working the late shift."

"Holiday hours," she says with a shrug. "Everybody wants their pies and rolls at the same time."

Her tone's breezy, but there's a tightness around her eyes that doesn't match it.

I glance at the bruise, then at her face. "You okay?"

She hesitates—barely a flicker—and then says, "Yeah, sure. Just clumsy. You know me."

I want to press. Ask what really happened. But there's a customer waiting, and I can feel her putting distance up like a wall.

"Right," I say. "You and gravity have a long history."

She laughs, light but fragile. "Exactly."

The old man pays and shuffles off. Sam wipes down the counter with a damp rag, eyes on her work.

"You playing this weekend?" she asks.

"Yeah. We've got Watertown for basketball next week. Should be a good game."

"You'll kill it," she says, smiling again.

I nod, pushing back from the counter. "Take care of yourself, Sam."

"You too, Robbie."

As I roll out, I glance back once. She's already turned to the next customer, shoulders hunched under the fluorescent light.

When I finally start the engine, I tell myself I'm just worried as a friend. That's all.

But the ache in my chest says otherwise.

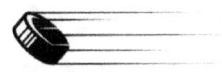

The next evening is one of my regular dinners at Carly's apartment. I'm still thinking about Sam and trying to figure out how to talk to her about whether she's safe and happy. I have no solution so my mind just keeps spinning on the topic over and over without making any progress. I'm surprised when I roll in that Murph isn't there. I rarely see them apart anymore.

"Where's the boyfriend?" I ask.

Carly is standing at the stove as usual, spatters of tomato sauce on her apron. I'm sure she'll be scrubbing it with bleach later. "He had to go to a board meeting," she says.

I don't know the ins and outs of how his sled hockey team officially works and I don't want to. Sounds incredibly boring. Which is why the whole non-profit bureaucracy thing is perfect for Carly.

"Come and sit down," she says, carrying two bowls to her table. I chuckle under my breath. It's just an expression but it never fails to amuse me when someone invites me to take a seat.

I look at the bowl and frown. "Soup?" I say.

"Trust me, it's hearty," Carly says. "Potato leek soup will fill up even you. And there's sourdough bread too." She pulls a basket closer to us and lifts the corner of a napkin to reveal thick white slices of bread.

So I pull out the strap for my hand that a spoon slots into and dig in. I savor the thick flavor and try not to think about anything else.

Through the window behind Carly I see yellow and red leaves falling. The trees are almost entirely bare now. I've appreciated these last several years that I didn't have to deal with snow to hang out with her but by this winter she'll be across town. She could come visit here, but if Murph wanted to come then there's going to be a wheeler who has to struggle through the snow, whether it's him or me.

"You seem quiet tonight, Robbie. What's going on?" That crease appears between her eyebrows—the one that's been there since we were kids, back when she used to worry if I stayed out past curfew. I hate that I put it there now. I'm not about to tell her what I was actually thinking, that her moving out feels like someone's slowly peeling away the last piece of "home" I've got. She doesn't need that kind of guilt.

I shrug. "Just thinking about Sam."

Her spoon stills mid-air. "Sam from the store?"

"Yeah."

"Anything in particular?"

I break a piece of bread between my fists and dip it into the soup. The crust goes soft in seconds. "You've noticed the bruises, right?"

"Yeah," she says quietly. "I have."

"I've never met her husband," I say. "Don't know a thing about the guy. But every time I see a new one...I just wonder. I want to ask, but how do you even do that? 'Hey, the person you go home to, do they hurt you?'" I shake my head. "If I'm wrong, I humiliate her. If I'm right..."

Carly leans back, temples her fingers together, lost in thought. The radiator clicks softly in the corner, filling the silence. I dip another chunk of bread and wait her out.

Finally she says, "What if we invite them over? You know, 'Friendsgiving.' We can see what he's like for ourselves. Might give us some context."

I look up at her, surprised by the simple genius of it. "That's...yeah. That's actually a great idea."

She grins. "Of course it is. I'm the smart one, remember?"

"You'd really do that?"

"Of course. Sam's my friend too."

I nod, a little relieved. Carly's good at reading people, she'll see what I can't.

She thinks I've got a crush on Sam. I've told her a dozen times it's not like that—but maybe it's not entirely *not* like that either. It's more complicated. I just want Sam safe. There's something in her eyes lately. A kind of faraway look, like she's keeping her spirit locked behind glass.

Carly's already zoning out, tapping her finger on her lip. I can tell she's mentally building a menu. "Okay," she murmurs, "Friendsgiving means finger foods, right? Maybe stuffed mushrooms, mini quiches, cranberry bars..."

I chuckle. "You're already planning it."

She shoots me a grin. "It's tradition: I overfeed people, you take home leftovers."

"Speaking of which," I say, lifting my bowl, "this soup's worth hoarding."

After dinner, we slip into our usual rhythm: she washes, I dry. It's automatic by now. When the counters are clear and the kitchen smells faintly of soap and cream, she packs up a cardboard box with Tupperware containers of soup and sets it on my lap.

"For your fridge," she says. "So you don't live off granola bars."

"Appreciate the charity," I say with a grin.

"Call it sibling duty."

I wheel backward out of her apartment, the warm air following me into the hall. The lights overhead buzz softly.

"Text me when you're home safe," she calls.

"I'm literally two floors away."

"Text anyway."

I laugh and let the elevator doors close between us. The ride is slow, the kind that hums just loud enough to give you time to think. The soup box balances on my knees. It's probably still warm but I can't tell.

When the doors open, the hallway is dim and still. I roll toward my apartment, the rubber of my tires whispering against the carpet. My key fob beeps, the lock clicks, and I nudge the door open with the side of my wheel.

The apartment greets me the way it always does: lamplight low and warm, the faint hum of the refrigerator, the gentle whir of the heater kicking on. I hang my jacket on the hook near the door. It slips off once before I manage to balance it right.

I unload the box of leftovers Carly packed for me and slide them into the fridge. The containers clack softly against the glass shelf. There's something comforting about how her food always takes up too much space in there, like she's watching over me somehow.

Carly and I have been doing this for too long. Passing leftovers, checking in, filling the gaps for each other. Ten years of it. It's just how our lives work. We've always relied on each other a little too much. I know that. We built this careful balance where she gets to be the responsible one and I get to be the one she worries about. It works. It's safe. But it's also...stuck.

I wheel toward the window, lift one slat of the blinds. My reflection in the glass stares back. Older, steadier, but still that same kid underneath, the one who thought he had it all figured out before the world spun off its axis.

The memory creeps in before I can stop it.

Music thumping in the distance. Wet pavement shining under the streetlight. My breath clouding in the cold as I sprint across the road, sneakers slapping the asphalt. Someone shouting my name behind me, laughing. Then headlights.

Too close. Too fast.

The sound of metal folding, glass breaking, the sudden quiet after.

It's strange, the things that stick: the smell of beer from the spilled bottle near my hand, the grit of gravel against my cheek, the way the streetlight above me looked fractured, doubled, like it couldn't decide which version of me to shine on.

And then waking up in a hospital room I didn't recognize, Carly crying in a chair she wouldn't leave. Mom praying. Dad trying not to.

When they said the word *quadriplegic,* I didn't know what to do with it. But Carly did. She took it and started building around it like she could make it make sense. She became my translator for everything I couldn't yet face.

She was twenty-one and supposed to be in grad school, not fighting with insurance companies or figuring out how to lift me into a car.

The rehab at Thatcher Memorial was temporary, but Cedar Harbor somehow became home for us. Mom and Dad went back to Pennsylvania for a while, then retired early and moved to Florida. Carly and I stayed. We said it was because we liked Cedar Harbor. But maybe it was because neither of us knew how to stop holding each other up.

I let the blinds fall closed and rub the back of my neck. My muscles ache from basketball practice earlier, but it's a good ache; one that reminds me how far I've come since those first months when I couldn't move my hands at all.

I know that Carly moving on is healthy. She deserves her own life, her own partner, her own space. I'm proud of her. But it also means that this thing we built—the quiet, easy codependence—is going to shift. And change, even when it's good, still hurts.

I roll to the bathroom, brush my teeth with the cuff around my hand, and rinse the sink clean. Then I wheel to the bed and transfer, one motion at a time: hands braced, elbows locked, shoulders burning.

The sheets are cool across my shoulders. The apartment hums softly around me. I stare at the ceiling for a while, tracing the faint shadows cast by the streetlight outside. But my routine demands attention and I can't wallow. Before falling asleep I have to do my skin check and stretches.

I lean to one side, propping myself on my elbow, and use the small mirror I keep on the nightstand to scan for red spots along my hips and thighs. All clear tonight. That's good. One less worry. When I'm done, I stretch. Shoulders first, slow rolls until I feel the pull through my arms, then triceps, neck, wrists. My joints crack softly, the sound sharp in the still air. I press my palms against the mattress to get a deeper stretch across my chest. It feels good, grounding. Finally, I lay back and push against the bed to turn my spine to one side then the other.

I check the temperature on my phone to make sure I've got the right blanket coverage. Another strange detail you only do when you can't feel most of your body. I flick a thin blanket over me and lie back again.

Sleep usually comes easily to me. I rarely stop moving so the moment I do, my body is ready to zonk out. Tonight is harder. I can't stop wondering what Friendsgiving with Sam will be like. I envision all kinds of different scenarios and different personalities for her husband. Even though I know it's useless, I just can't stop.

Samantha

My life isn't what I pictured, but whose is? When we're young, we draw neat maps of the future: where we'll live, who we'll love, what our days will look like. Then life unfolds in its own crooked handwriting.

The rag in my hand leaves damp streaks across the bookshelf. Will's at his computer, the glow from the monitor flickering over his face. His mouse clicks in a steady rhythm, quick little bursts, the way it always does when he's doing his fantasy sports thing. I was going to vacuum, but he complained about the noise, so here I am, dusting around the picture frames instead.

I pause, cloth in hand, and watch him for a moment. The way his shoulders hunch forward, the little frown line between his brows. I remember that face younger, happier, under a string of dollar-store lights on our wedding day. We laughed until I cried. He'd kissed me like I was a promise.

Now his jaw twitches as he clicks. My chest tightens with something that feels like affection—or maybe just the ghost of it. I want that day back, or at least the version of me who believed in it.

If he would just get help, maybe we could still find that version of ourselves. He carries guilt around like a second skin, and I know therapy could help, but he won't go. Says it's a scam. Says it's for weak people. And anyway, we couldn't afford it even if he agreed.

"I'm sorry things have been rough lately," Will says suddenly. He doesn't turn, but his voice softens just enough to make me hopeful.

I smile faintly. "Thank you."

He clicks the mouse a few more times, then adds, "I'm under stress and you always make it worse."

The warmth drains out of me.

I stare at the grain of the wood under my cloth, tracing it with the rag. I don't ask what's stressing him. He doesn't work. The rental property handles itself, and the only real obligations he has are his mother's phone calls. Maybe she's been at him again about his life, about me. I try not to add to his stress, but it feels like my very breathing irritates him.

When he looks at me, I sometimes get the sense that if he could, he'd turn a knob and just...switch me off. Tuck me in the closet until he wanted something.

He exhales sharply, muttering about a missed score. I turn away before he notices I've been watching.

The quiet stretches, broken only by the hum of the fridge and the tapping of his mouse. My mind drifts back, unspooling like an old film reel.

When I was little, the women at The Foundation said a good wife never brought burden to her husband. They used to grade us on our lessons, the ones about gentleness and obedience. I always hovered near the bottom. I asked too many questions.

I remember the day I found *The Hobbit* hidden in a storage room behind the prayer books. The cover was worn, the pages soft from other forbidden hands. I read it in secret, heart hammering, feeling like I was holding something alive. I read it again and again until I knew the sentences by heart.

It wasn't even the story itself—it was the idea that there *was* another world out there, one not written by our leaders.

Outside the community, we were told, people were lost. They chased pleasure instead of Truth. They were selfish, empty, damned. I pitied them. Honestly pitied them. I can still hear myself agreeing when the women whispered that the girl who ran away was weak, not devoted enough.

It makes me sick to remember it now. The smug certainty of it. I thought we were pure. I thought we were safe. If we did everything as we were told, did everything right, God would love us.

But the trick is, there is no way to do everything right.

I keep wiping the same spot on the shelf, my hand moving automatically. Some of those beliefs are still inside me, deep down, quiet as seeds in frozen ground. I never know when one might sprout again, some old reflex about obedience, about how women should be small and silent and grateful.

"Why are you just standing there looking dumb?" Will's voice snaps me out of it.

"I wasn't," I murmur, and turn toward the kitchen. The dishwater is warm, and the scent of lemon soap fills the air. I focus on that: the feel of the sponge, the bubbles sticking to my forearms, the sound of plates clinking against the sink. Small things I can control.

You probably think I'm pathetic. Maybe I am. I don't even argue anymore. It's safer not to. Strong women are adored in stories, but in real life they get punished.

Sometimes, in the quiet after one of his moods, I catch myself wondering what the point of it all is. I'm nobody special. Just a woman keeping herself alive one polite smile at a time.

Still, I keep going.

I make Will's meals. I coax smiles from strangers at the grocery store. I remember people's names and ask about their dogs. I build tiny moments of kindness like stacking stones across a river, one step at a time.

Maybe that's enough.

It's not the life I imagined when I ran from the cult, but it's better than that cage. The world they warned me about—the sinful one—it's complicated and messy, yes, but people here find their own ways to be good. To be divine. That was The Foundation's biggest lie, that goodness only lived in one place.

But leaving wasn't as simple as packing a bag and walking away. You don't just lose your faith; you lose your compass. Your name. Your family. Everything that told you who you were.

Sometimes I still don't know who I am without them.

The memory that broke me comes back sharp: I was sixteen, accused of stealing a bottle of wine meant for the elders. I hadn't touched it, but when I denied it, no one cared. The woman accusing me was higher in the hierarchy—her word weighed more than mine.

We were supposed to value Truth above all else. That's what they always said. But when I saw how quickly everyone turned away, how easily the idea of truth bent under power...that was the first crack.

I apologized like they told me to, but the seed of doubt had already split open inside me.

By the time they started arranging my marriage, I knew if I didn't run then, I never would. So I left. I ran into a world I didn't understand. I've been trying to piece myself together ever since.

The back door bangs shut. I glance up from the sink and see Will's fishing rod is no longer leaning against the wall. The sudden quiet settles over the kitchen like a warm blanket. I rest my wet hands on the counter and close my eyes.

For the first time all day, the house feels peaceful.

Robbie

Carly's apartment looks like it's been swallowed by cardboard. Boxes are stacked against the wall, some half-packed, some already taped shut and labeled in her neat handwriting—*Books, Winter Clothes, Kevin's Tools (Do Not Touch)*. The air smells faintly of packing tape and dust.

I've parked myself in the corner by the window with my knees angled out just enough to keep clear of her path. My official job title? *Moral support and supervisor.* In other words, I watch her stress-pack while pretending I'm helping.

Carly moves methodically, wrapping things in newspaper, humming under her breath. The only sound besides that is the crinkle of paper and the faint thump of a box closing. She's in one of her focused moods—lips pursed, brow furrowed, the same look she gets balancing budgets or planning holiday dinners.

So I fill the silence for her.

"Did I tell you about Darius's epic wipeout at practice?" I say. "He tried to do a one-handed spin shot and somehow ended up on his back with both wheels in the air. Claimed it was part of his new 'defensive strategy.'"

Carly snorts without looking up. "I'm sure the other team was *terrified*."

"Of course they were," I say. "Mostly because we almost had to call 911 when he couldn't get his seatbelt unhooked."

Her laughter fills the room: small, genuine, exactly what I was going for. I love that sound. For ten years now, it's been one of my favorite things: proof that she's still here, still okay, after everything.

I'm about to launch into another story when it happens—a sudden jolt through my body, a sharp pull in my lower back. My legs twitch involuntary, and the back of my chair catches me as the spasm ripples through.

For a split second, my whole focus narrows to that electric tightening in my thighs. Not pain; more like my body's way of tapping on the glass and saying *hey, something's up.*

"Damn," I mutter under my breath, pressing my wrist to my thigh. I don't get spasms much, which means this one has a message. And after a decade, I know exactly which message that is.

"I'll be right back," I tell Carly, keeping my tone light.

She waves absently, still elbow-deep in a box of photo albums. "Sure thing."

The bathroom door clicks shut behind me. The space is small but familiar; she set it up years ago with wide enough clearance for my chair and a low shelf where I keep a few supplies. I hook my wrist around the handle of the cabinet and tug it open. My catheter kit sits in its usual spot.

Opening the package takes finesse. I brace the corner of the wrapper against the edge of the counter and tear it open using my wrist and the side of my fist. The plastic crinkles loud in the small room. I've done this so many times that my body moves through it automatically now.

By the time I roll back into the living room, Carly's crouched in front of the bookshelf, staring at the last empty shelf like it just insulted her.

"You okay?" I ask, stopping beside her.

She doesn't answer right away, just keeps looking at that shelf like it's a symbol of something bigger. "Yeah," she says finally. "Just...thinking."

I know that tone. "Nervous about Murph meeting Mom and Dad?"

She gives a small, guilty smile. "Maybe a little."

I tilt my head. "You've never brought anyone home before."

"I know." She sits back on her heels, picking at a loose thread on her sleeve. "It's not like I didn't date. I just...never felt like anyone was serious enough. Or good enough."

"For you, or for them?" I ask.

Her mouth curves into a smirk. "Don't psychoanalyze me, Robbie."

"Isn't that what you asked me here for?" I tease and she rolls her eyes.

Then she exhales, glancing toward the window. "How do you think they'll react?"

"To Murph?" I shrug. "You know that he's good for you and what mom and dad think is irrelevant."

She laughs. "If only it really were that simple."

It can be. She puts too much pressure on herself to please other people. The curse of being the older sibling, probably. I'm the reckless one and she's the responsible one. Roles people could tell we fit into from the time we were babies.

"Looks like that shelf's done," I say, breaking the silence. "What's next?"

"Well, I'm leaving the kitchen for last," she says. "So maybe the bedroom."

"Ah," I say, pretending to shudder. "The danger zone. That's my cue to make a graceful exit."

She rolls her eyes. "You're a terrible helper."

"I prefer 'excellent supervisor,'" I say, giving her a wink.

She laughs again, shaking her head. "Go on then. I know where to find you if I need moral support."

"You always do."

I turn my chair toward the door, and as I roll into the hallway, my chest feels tight. I'm not going to tell Carly but it's time for me to visit Sam at the grocery store. I look forward to these times and I wouldn't miss it for anything.

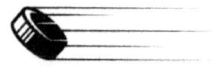

At this time of year the weather can't make up its mind. Some mornings there's a layer of frost on the truck windshield, and other days I roll outside and the air feels soft, almost springlike. Today's one of those warmer ones. The pavement's damp, smelling faintly of rain and wet leaves.

Winter's always a mixed bag for me. I'm grateful Cedar Harbor keeps the sidewalks clear—our snowplow guy deserves a medal—but salt gets ground into my tires and crusts on the hubs. A chore for another day. For now, the streets glisten, and the air on my face feels clean and alive. When sensation only reaches certain parts of your body, you learn to savor what's left.

By the time I reach the grocery store, I can already see Sam down the first aisle, restocking shelves. Her brown hair's half pulled up, and the rest tumbles over her striped cardigan like the world's softest waterfall.

For a second, I stay where I am, watching her move: quick, precise, humming something I can't quite catch. Then I roll closer, catching her attention just before she reaches for a misplaced box of cereal.

"The best time to wear a striped sweater," I announce, "is all the time."

She blinks, mid-reach. "What?"

"SpongeBob," I say, as if that explains everything.

Her brows draw together, and she shakes her head. "Oh—I've never seen it."

I feign shock. "What?! How is that possible?"

She tucks a strand of hair behind her ear, looking sheepish. "My parents were really strict. Homeschooled me. We didn't have TV."

Something flickers behind her tone—hesitation, like she's said too much. I could press, but I don't. I've learned not to chase people's pain before they hand it to you willingly.

"I've seen every episode multiple times," I say instead.

Her laugh bursts out, bright and light, like the shake of small bells. "You are such a classic all-American."

"Guilty," I say with a grin. "Not a care in the world—until this happened." I tap the rim of my wheel with the side of my fist.

It's true. Life was simple and clear up until the accident that threw me completely off course. I think back for a moment to my high school days. I was popular, friends with everyone at school. I knew the name of every student there. I was a star in every sport I tried. I was thinking about college and the plans for the rest of my life. Then I went to a party on a fateful weekend and on the way home got ploughed into by a drunk driver.

Things got a lot more complicated for me after that. My whole future changed. Now I work phones as a customer service rep. Not what I had envisioned but I never did make it to college.

I tried to say it lightly, but her eyes hold mine in that steady, quiet way she has, and for a moment, the air between us feels heavy with something unspoken.

I wonder what her childhood was like. I could imagine her eating with a group of girls in the cafeteria, cheering at football games all bundled up in winter coat and hat. But she said she was homeschooled so my vision probably isn't accurate.

Her shift-manager calls something from the front, and she glances over her shoulder. When she turns back, her expression's thoughtful, almost shy. "I'm due for a break. Do you want to come sit outside with me?"

That catches me off guard. We've talked a hundred times in this store, but this is different. An invitation. I nod before I can overthink it.

She leads the way through the back door. Behind the building, the parking lot stretches out mostly empty and sun-bleached. A single picnic table sits by the dumpster, half in shadow, half in sunlight. Sam sits on the bench, and for once she's almost eye-level with me. She folds her hands on the table, her smile fading a little. There's a tiredness in her eyes I haven't noticed before. I don't know how to ask about it so I don't. It's over my head (and these days most things are...ba-dum-bum).

"I've never seen someone have dimples on their forehead," Sam says. She reaches out and lifts my hair, touching her fingertips to one of the two dents in my forehead. I take a deep breath and try to ignore the sudden longing in my skin.

"That's because they aren't dimples, they're scars," I say.

Her hand freezes, then drops. "What?"

I nod. "Yeah when you break your neck you have to a wear a brace for a while that's called a halo and it's screwed into your head to keep your spine stable."

"I didn't know that."

"It's not the kind of thing you know about before it happens to you," I say with a laugh.

"It must have been very hard to adjust to being in a wheelchair."

"It was. But I got through it. Everyone has challenges in their life and I've gotten used to mine."

"I have a scar too," Sam says after a moment. She holds out her left hand and turns it so I can see the side below her thumb. The skin there is wrinkled and whiter than the rest of her skin.

"What happened?" I prompt.

"I was making coffee at 4:00 in the morning and I reached over a kettle that was steaming."

"Wait, I'm missing something. You don't drink coffee and why so early?"

She dips her head and tucks a strand of brown hair behind her ear. "I don't usually tell people this," she begins, "but I want you to know the truth."

I suddenly feel alarmed. What is she about to tell me? I stay quiet and wait for her to continue. She looks out across the parking lot and says, "I grew up in a religious cult."

"A *cult* cult?!" I didn't mean to interrupt but it's my turn to be shocked.

She nods. "As a girl I was a server and one of my duties was to bring coffee to the higher ups in the morning. A server is basically a wife-training role. All the teenage girls do it."

My heart is in my throat at this point but I let her continue.

"I didn't even know the kettle was turned on. I reached across the top of it for a mug and the steam burned my hand. For a while no one believed me but then a huge blister puffed up on my hand and cold water only stopped the pain for a few moments. The other girls said I was faking it to get out of work. I didn't go to a doctor but there was a woman trained as a nurse who treated it. Everyone laughed at me for being so stupid to not know the kettle was hot but the steam wasn't even showing yet when it happened."

"I'm so sorry," I say, not knowing anything else to say. I can't believe the adults just made fun of her and didn't bring her to a doctor.

She gives me a weak smile. and says, "Thank you."

"This was happening around here?"

Sam nods. "Cults are all around," she says quietly. "You'd be shocked if you knew how many there are."

I'm sure I would. I always thought of cults as something far away, in a different world from mine. Then again, I used to think that way about wheelchairs and disability too.

She glances toward the building, checking her phone. "Break's over."

We wheel and walk back toward the store, neither of us speaking. The automatic doors hiss open, spilling us back into fluorescent light.

I try to find words, any words, but what comes out is, "How's your husband doing?"

Her smile tightens. "He's okay." She looks at the floor as she says it.

Something cold slides down my spine.

I can tell she's going to change the subject so I quickly say, "My sister wanted to invite you and him to her place for a little friendsgiving. Maybe the week after Thanksgiving?"

"Oh!" Sam looks up again and I see that sparkle in her eye that I love. "That sounds wonderful."

I feel a bit torn. I want to get to see her outside of work and I feel like I need to know more about Will. But Carly is right, I do have feelings for Sam and hanging out with her and her husband is going to be tough on my emotions.

"So I can tell her yes?" I say.

"I'll see what Will thinks," she says and then bites the corner of her lip absentmindedly.

We go through a few more aisles and my list is almost complete. "Guess what?" I say.

"What?" Again her face lights up and makes me smile.

"I brought you another book."

"Show me!"

"Okay, but you have to promise you're not going to think less of me as a man when you see it."

She laughs. "Never," she promises.

I hook my arm over the back of my wheelchair so I can lean over without falling and start working the book out of the mesh bag under my chair. After a few moments of using the side of my hand to push the book, it finally falls out onto the floor.

"Sorry," I say as Sam bends over and scoops it up.

"No worries," she says brightly, turning the book over in her hands. It's Pride & Prejudice. I know, I know. But it's a great book and it's funny, sharp and witty.

"I've always wanted to read this," Sam says. "Thank you!"

For a moment it seems like she's going to lean over and hug me but instead she just rocks up onto her toes.

"Well, I'm off to hockey practice," I say and the moment feels awkward. "Maybe you'd like to come see the next one?"

"I would love that," she says.

As I roll toward the exit, the automatic doors open and the late-afternoon light pours in—golden and soft. Behind me, I can still hear her humming under her breath, the same tune from before, carrying me out into the fading warmth.

The rink air has that sharp metallic cold that cuts right through my sweatshirt. The overhead lights glare down on the ice, throwing white reflections across the smooth surface like frozen lightning. My breath clouds in front of me, faint and steady.

Danny crouches beside me, one glove braced on the ice for balance. "Ready?" he asks.

"Born ready," I say.

Danny steadies the sled as I shift my weight and slowly lower myself in. He tightens the straps and gives the backrest a small pat. "Good?"

"Good."

He nods, pushes off the boards, and glides backward effortlessly. Show-off.

People who aren't disabled tend to think of us as one big category: *wheelchair user* is all they see. But in this world, there's a whole unspoken hierarchy. Paraplegics like Danny and amputees like Murph can use their full arms, transfer fast, control their chairs with ease. Then there's guys like me: low-level quadriplegic, weaker arms, no grip, everything slower and more deliberate. And then there are folks even further down the line, the ones who can't push a manual chair. We're about to meet someone on that tier.

Danny flicks the puck toward me, the sound crisp in the cold air. I catch it between my sticks. Then the sharp rap of knuckles on metal breaks the rhythm.

An older woman's voice floats through the doorway. "Excuse me?"

Murph, who's closest to the boards, pivots fast, slicing sideways to a stop. A spray of ice fans out at his sides. "Hey there," he calls, all friendly ease. "Can I help you?"

Danny and I both turn our heads to watch. The woman steps into the room, clutching her purse strap like she's not sure she's supposed to be here. Behind her, a motor hums.

A power chair rolls in slowly. The young guy driving it looks barely twenty, maybe just a teen, dark hair falling over his forehead, shoulders hunched a little. His hand rests lightly on the joystick, guiding it with practiced care.

"My son Mark was interested in your hockey team," the woman says.

Murph's face brightens. "Awesome! Great to meet you, Mark." He moves his sled closer, his tone switching to coach mode. "You ever done adaptive sports before?"

Mark shakes his head, then answers softly, "No." His voice is clear but hesitant, the kind of voice that hasn't had much practice being the center of attention.

"That's totally fine," Murph says. "We all start somewhere."

His mom glances between us and the ice, uneasy. "We weren't sure if he could participate, with his level of disability."

Murph nods. "We'll make it work. We're not out here for trophies. We're out here to play."

Then to us: "Keep practicing, guys. I'll be right back."

He unclips from his sled, props his hands on the boards, and transfers fluidly into his everyday chair before rolling over to talk with Mark.

Danny leans toward me. "Think he's giving the speech?"

I grin. "You mean the 'everyone belongs on the ice' speech?"

"That's the one. Let's make sure we're doing something worth showing off."

He sends the puck my way, hard and fast. I catch it on the blade and flick it back, the sound ringing out like a gunshot in the open rink. The cold air doesn't touch me below the chest, but I can still feel the vibration of each push through my shoulders and arms, a rhythm I never get tired of.

We skate back and forth: passing, turning, laughing when we mess up. I glimpse Murph on the sidelines, leaning in close to talk with Mark and his mom. He gestures toward the sleds, explaining something about straps and support. Mark listens intently, eyes wide, the faintest hint of a smile forming.

It's hard to imagine how he'll manage on the ice. But that's not my call to make. If there's one thing I've learned since the accident, it's that "impossible" usually just means "not yet adapted."

When Murph finally rolls back, his grin says everything. He transfers back into his sled, tightens his straps, and claps his gloves together. "Okay," he says. "Let's run some drills."

Danny gives me a quick side-eye. "No news?"

Murph just smirks. "Maybe next time."

We line up again. "Two-on-one," he calls. "Robbie, you're goalie."

"Always me," I groan.

"Because you've got the best instincts," he says, already sliding toward me.

The puck flies. I block it with the blade of my stick, send it skidding back toward Danny, who whoops as he chases it down.

From the doorway, Mark watches every move. His mom stands behind him, one hand on his shoulder. His smile's bigger now, his eyes shining with something I recognize: that flicker of *I could do this.*

I hope he gets to try. Because that first time you glide across the ice, it changes something deep inside you.

Samantha

Robbie invited me to watch one of his hockey practices, and with Will gone all weekend on a fishing trip, I said yes before I could talk myself out of it.

I try not to think too much about what being around Robbie does to me. He's kind, funny, gentle in a way that sneaks up on me. And it's not about romance. It's just nice to feel...safe. Relaxed. Seen. That's a luxury these days. Still, every time I laugh too easily in his presence, or my chest feels lighter, a tiny sting of guilt follows.

I lock the front door behind me and pull my long sweater tighter around me. The air is soft today, the kind of false spring that sneaks into late November. Snow still carpets the ground, but the temperature has climbed to the fifties. After days of icy wind, the damp warmth feels almost indulgent.

The three-mile walk to the rink is quiet. The trees lining the trail are still heavy with snow, their branches bending under the weight. Droplets fall in slow rhythm as the ice melts, splashing my boots. The air smells like wet pine and salt. It's peaceful. I can't remember the last time I took a walk like this just for myself.

By the time I reach the gym, the sound of scraping blades and echoing laughter fills the space. I spot Robbie immediately. He's out on the ice, gliding across the rink in that low, steady rhythm of the sled. There's no hesitation in his movements, only strength and control. For someone who lives in a chair, he looks completely free out there.

I scan the bleachers and spot Carly sitting halfway up. Her red scarf stands out against the pale wood. She gives me a friendly wave and pats the space beside her, though there's a flicker of wariness in her eyes. I can't blame her. She probably wonders what, exactly, I am to her brother. I wish I knew the answer myself.

I sit down next to her. "Hey," I say, a little breathless. "They've already started?"

"Warm-ups," she says, smiling. "They always start early."

We watch together as the guys move across the ice. Carly points out each person. "You know Robbie. The captain there is my boyfriend, Kevin. Then there's Danny. You've probably met him, he does all the handy work around town. The last one is new, Mark. He just joined a few days ago."

The game starts as a small skirmish: Kevin and Mark versus Robbie and Danny. I lean forward, drawn in immediately. Each man sits in a sleek sled with a blade under the seat like an ice skate. They have two short hockey sticks with spikes on one end for propulsion. Robbie's sticks are strapped to his arms, so he moves with this sharp, rhythmic precision—dig, pull, glide, shoot. The sound of metal on ice rings out crisp and clean.

Kevin moves fast, his upper body pumping like a machine, switching from speed to control in a blink. Danny laughs as he blocks him, the sound carrying across the rink. Robbie, though—he's pure focus. Determination and joy rolled into one. I can't stop watching him. There's light in his eyes I've never seen before.

Carly answers my quiet questions, describing the rules, explaining how the gear works. Her voice blends with the scrape of blades, the clang of the puck against the boards, the laughter that fills the cold space.

It's beautiful, really. There's power and grace in all of it. I try to picture Will like this: alive, energized, surrounded by people who lift him up instead of drag him down. I can't. The closest he comes to joy is when he's on the water, fishing alone, unreachable. And he never asks me to join him.

I shouldn't compare them. It isn't fair. But the contrast is impossible to ignore. Robbie radiates something warm and open that I didn't realize I missed so much until now.

When the practice ends, the sound of laughter echoes off the boards as the players slow to a stop. Robbie turns toward the bleachers, his smile catching me off guard. I wave, my heart doing something it shouldn't.

I make myself keep it short. "Great game," I say when I step up to the edge of the rink as he's packing up. "You looked—" *Happy,* I almost say, but catch myself. "—really good out there."

He grins. "Thanks. You should come watch again."

I mumble something about maybe, then excuse myself before Carly can give me that knowing look.

Outside, the air is cooling again, the sky going pink around the edges. I take the long way home. For once, the quiet feels kind instead of lonely.

Will comes home late Sunday night, smelling of lake water and cigarettes. He doesn't ask how my weekend was, and I don't volunteer that I spent part of it at a hockey rink.

By Monday morning, I've already started packing our suitcases for Thanksgiving. I clean out the fridge, put a hold on the mail, and fold our clothes neatly into the old leather bags his mother gave us years ago.

When he walks through the door that afternoon, he doesn't thank me. Just looks around and says, "You're ready? Good. I hate waiting."

The drive north to his mother's house feels endless. Will flicks through radio stations, muttering about politics, criticizing every voice that comes through the speakers. I try to focus on my sewing project—just a spool of thread and a few buttons to tighten—but the car jolts too much. Each time I prick my finger, I flinch, and he snaps, "Stop fidgeting." After the third time, I fold the fabric into my lap and stare out the window instead.

The landscape slides by: gray trees, patches of melting snow, the dull gleam of water between them. My reflection stares back from the glass: pale, tired, trying too hard.

Edwina's house sits near the border of Massachusetts and New Hampshire, a grand old colonial with too many rooms and not enough warmth. She greets us at the door in a cloud of perfume and disapproval. "You're late," she says to me, as if I were driving.

Inside, Will brightens immediately, slipping back into the role of perfect son. I fade into the background, like furniture.

That night, I wander upstairs while they talk in the den. The main floor walls are spotless—no photos, no trace of family life—but upstairs the hallways are lined with frames. Smiling faces, childhood summers, holidays before the accident that killed his little brother, when Will had a happy life.. There's a picture of Will as a teenager, laughing beside a boy who must be Michael. Will's arm is thrown around him, his grin open and easy. I stop in front of it for a long time. I wish I could have met that version of my husband. The man he would have become if tragedy hadn't struck.

When he comes to bed later, I'm already half asleep. He reaches for me in the dark, impatient, and I try not to stiffen, try not to think about the fact that his mother is just two doors away. We have nothing else connecting us anymore; sex is the last thread holding our marriage together. I let him take what he wants. I think he enjoys it even more in his childhood home. Sneaking it in seems to give him a rush.

Thanksgiving Day.

The dining room smells of green beans and starch. The table is beautiful but bare: no centerpiece, no candles, just a small spread of food that wouldn't fill two plates. Strangely there's never enough food when we eat with his mother. Edwina chronically underestimates what is reasonable to feed people and she excuses it with the statement that "people are too fat these days anyway." Dinner with her always leaves me hungry but it's even more remarkable that it happens even on Thanksgiving when feasting is expected.

"A little restraint builds character," Edwina says primly as she spoons the beans onto her plate.

I smile politely and push my turkey around.

"Will has such a sensitive heart," she says, looking at him with pride. "You know, his last girlfriend before you was completely unhinged after the breakup. The poor thing was obsessed. But Will, he was so compassionate about it. He has this innate sense of what people need to hear."

I know the story. I've heard it a dozen times. The "compassionate" thing he said to that girl was that she was too ugly to be with him. But here, in this house, the truth doesn't matter.

Will beams under her praise, soaking it in.

I can't help but remember the first fight of our marriage when he slammed me into a wall for disrespecting him and got angry at me for keeping him awake with my crying in the guest room. We called Edwina because she is, believe it or not, a marriage counselor. She told us that I have a weak spirit and Will must be firm with me. It's his sacred duty to keep me in line.

It shouldn't have surprised me that she was always going to take his side.

After dinner, I help clear the dishes. Neither of them thanks me.

When we finally get back in the car to drive home, I can't hide the sigh that escapes me. Will flips through the radio again, landing on a talk show host who's yelling about the economy. I tune it all out and look at the horizon instead.

The thought that keeps me steady isn't noble or profound. It's simple: Robbie's Friendsgiving is coming up. A night with warmth, laughter, and people who see me as something more than a mistake someone made.

For once, I have something to look forward to.

Robbie

Mom and Dad arrive like a winter storm. They sweep into Carly's apartment in a flurry of bags, scarves, and overlapping voices. Mom's curls bounce with every movement as she takes immediate command of the small space. Her coat's only half-off before she's refolding the napkins Carly carefully laid out an hour ago.

Dad lingers behind her, coughing into his hand. His winter hat's still pulled halfway down his forehead as he claps me on the shoulder. "How are you holding up, son?"

"I'm good, Dad. No worries."

It's not new, that question, but the pity in his eyes never really fades. It's like every visit resets the clock. He forgets I've built a life around this body until he sees the chair again and the grief hits him fresh. I feel bad for him, honestly. There's no easy way to lose the version of your kid you imagined.

Mom's voice carries from the kitchen. "So when do we get to meet this mystery man of yours?"

Carly's folding and unfolding a dishtowel that doesn't need it. "He should be here any minute."

Her voice sounds calm, but her foot is tapping. Carly's always been the picture of composure, but when she's nervous, she vibrates like a string pulled too tight. Everything's already done: table set, food warming, music softly looping in the background, so there's nothing left for her to fuss with except her own thoughts.

I think about turning on the game to fill the silence, but before I can reach for the remote, the door opens.

Murph rolls in.

No prosthetics.

He's in his wheelchair, his sleek, carbon-fiber one, the same chair he uses every day. His muscular arms rest lightly on the push rims as he glides over the threshold. For a split second, the air in the room shifts. Mom's smile falters just slightly, her surprise barely masked before she recovers.

"Kevin!" she says, stepping forward quickly. "It's so nice to finally meet you."

Murph's smile is easy, confident. "You too, Mrs. Jennings." He offers a hand up for her to shake, and she does, though she's clearly recalibrating her expectations.

From my spot near the couch, I watch the exchange. I'm proud of Murph. He's serious about Carly and this is a tough moment to allow himself to not hide or minimize his vulnerabilities. I can tell he's self-conscious but only because I know him well.

He wheels further in, and Mom steps aside to let Dad shake his hand. "Good to meet you, sir," Murph says. Dad's eyes can't stop darting to the empty wheelchair seat where legs should be. I can see the tiny twitch at the corner of Murph's jaw, the effort it takes to stay easygoing while someone is sizing up your worth through a lens they don't even realize they're using.

Dad's grip is firm. "Likewise. Heard a lot about you."

Carly's still by the table, smiling with that mix of relief and affection that only she gets when she looks at Murph. The moment he meets her eyes, her shoulders drop half an inch.

"Come sit," she says, bustling toward him as if she needs to *do* something. She pulls a regular dining chair aside to make space for his wheels. "We've got plenty of room."

That's not true at all but no one calls her out on it. I hope the new place has a real dining room with plenty of space for Carly to entertain.

Once everyone settles, the apartment fills with the sound of plates clinking and chairs shifting. It's cozy but crowded. Carly's table wasn't meant for this many people, but she's somehow fit a Thanksgiving's worth of food onto it anyway: turkey glistening with butter, mashed sweet potatoes smooth as silk, honey-glazed carrots, and gravy that smells like heaven.

Mom sits beside Murph, trying not to stare as he deftly carves the turkey and passes pieces onto plates. I can almost see her mind racing to rewrite the story she expected to tell her friends later.

But Murph handles everything beautifully. He talks easily, asking her about her flight, about Florida winters versus New England ones. Within ten minutes, Mom's laughing again, the tension gone.

We eat mostly in silence after that; Carly's food deserves reverence. She's always been like this: a perfectionist at work, a caretaker at home. Every dish on the table tastes like effort and love and a little bit of showing off.

Halfway through, Dad leans back and wipes his mouth. "So, Kevin," he says. "You served, right? Army?"

"Yes, sir," Murph says. "EOD—Explosive Ordnance Disposal."

Dad's eyes light with recognition. "Engineering corps myself. Gulf War. So you know your way around equipment."

Murph nods. "Guess that's why I like adaptive sports so much. It's just a different kind of engineering. Problem-solving in motion."

Carly beams. I can tell she's proud. My parents are rapt, listening as Murph talks about coaching sled hockey, about customizing sleds for different body types and injuries. They don't linger on the IED, which I know Murph appreciates. For once, everything feels...easy.

I glance at Carly—she's glowing. Murph fits. He really does.

The conversation shifts to Carly's upcoming move and the new condo. Dad's nodding, impressed. Mom's making approving noises. But then she turns to me.

"And you, sweetheart?" she says. "If Carly moves across town, you can't be here all alone. What if something happens?"

The question lands heavy, though she doesn't mean it to.

"I'll be fine, Mom," I say. "We've talked about this."

"Still," she says, her brow knitting. "Maybe you could come down to Florida for a while. Just until you find someone to help. It would be good for you to be near family."

I can't help but smile at that—*near family* meaning *under supervision.*

"Just get me one of those medical alert buttons," I joke. "If I fall and can't get up, Carly will come running."

"Absolutely I will," Carly says, laughing.

Murph joins in easily. "Family comes first. We'll make sure he's got what he needs."

Something in Mom's face softens at that. She gives Murph a small, approving nod. It's clear she's decided he's a good man. The kind of man who takes care of people.

The tension ebbs away, replaced by the low hum of conversation and the clatter of silverware. Even Dad relaxes enough to lean back and pat his stomach.

Mom says, "This was wonderful, Carly. You've outdone yourself."

Carly smiles at the praise, cheeks pink from relief.

Friendsgiving is all set up, and somehow I'm the one who's nervous, not Carly. My stomach's tight, my shoulders ache from tension I can't shake off. Carly keeps telling me it's going to be fine, that everyone's just coming to eat good food and enjoy themselves, but that only makes it worse. I want this to go *well*.

I'm looking forward to seeing Sam again, of course. But I'm also curious about Will. Maybe he'll be great, I tell myself. Maybe he's one of those loud, funny guys who just says dumb things sometimes. Maybe we'll all end up friends. I can almost picture it: me, Murph, and Will yelling at the TV during football games, taking the ferry out to Georges Island for a day trip, poker nights where Carly and Sam roll their eyes from the kitchen. Yeah, it sounds like a sitcom. But let me have my fantasy.

The apartment smells amazing: garlic, rosemary, and something buttery that makes me wish I'd skipped lunch. Carly's gone full out, the way she always does. She's in host mode, fluttering around the kitchen in her soft gray sweater, hair tied up with a clip, looking calm but moving like she's got a clock ticking in her head.

Murph rolls up beside me at the table, his chair angled so he's half-facing me. "You look like you're about to go into a playoff game," he says.

"Feels like it," I admit. "My stomach's doing somer-
saults."

He grins. "Then I'll run interference if it gets weird."

That earns a half-laugh from me, which is good because
my mouth's been twitching, my go-to tell when I'm nervous. I can't tap my foot, can't fidget with my hands, so
all the anxiety just builds in my face. Murph catches it
and starts talking hockey to distract me: strategies for our
next match, how he wants to train the new kid to handle
cross-ice passes. It helps...for about two minutes.

Then there's a knock.

Carly straightens like she's been hit with an electric cur-
rent. She smooths her sweater, checks the table one more
time, and hurries to the door.

When it opens, my breath catches.

Sam stands there in dark jeans and a soft red T-shirt, hair
loose around her shoulders. She looks... different. Not like
the Sam from the grocery store...lighter somehow, though
that might just be the warm color of the room catching her
skin. She smiles when she sees me, that same gentle, bright
smile that always feels like it's aimed straight into my chest.

And next to her is Will.

He's not what I pictured. I don't know what I *did*
picture. Maybe a big outdoorsy guy? But Will is shorter,
stockier, maybe in his forties. His dark hair's thinning at

the temples, and his jaw looks permanently set, like he's chewing on irritation.

He looks around the apartment with the cool detachment of a man scanning for flaws.

Carly offers a bright "Hi! Come in, come in!" and takes their coats before the silence can stretch.

Will steps forward and sticks out his hand to me. "Robbie, right?"

"Yeah," I say, lifting my arm a little awkwardly. "Good to meet you."

When I raise my fist for the modified handshake I always do, confusion flashes across his face. He hesitates, then wraps his whole hand around mine and gives it one stiff shake, as though he's doing me a favor.

Sam jumps in before it can get more awkward. "This is Kevin," she says, turning toward him. "The one I told you about, the hockey player."

Murph grins and gives a small salute from his chair. "Welcome to the madhouse."

Sam laughs genuinely, the sound bright and easy but Will just nods, his eyes already flicking toward the food spread across the table.

The apartment feels smaller with six people and two wheelchairs. Carly squeezes around us, narrating every dish as she always does. "We've got rosemary roast chicken, garlic mashed potatoes, maple-glazed carrots, and home-made cranberry sauce made with fresh Cape cranberries..."

Will's mouth twists before she even finishes.

I glance at Carly, praying she didn't catch it, but Will leans closer to Sam and mutters, "Did you not tell them how I feel about homemade cranberry sauce?"

His voice isn't quiet enough. Murph's head turns slightly; I can tell he heard too.

"It must have slipped my mind," Sam says quickly, her voice soft and apologetic.

He rolls his eyes. "What do you have in that head of yours, a salad strainer?"

My pulse spikes. Carly freezes mid-motion, the serving spoon hovering over the potatoes.

"It's okay, sweetie," Sam says quietly. She touches his knee and moves the cranberry sauce onto her own plate. "I'll eat yours, then." She smiles at all of us like nothing happened, her tone bright, her shoulders relaxed. She's done this before.

Murph and I make eye contact across the table. His jaw's tight. Mine is too.

Will chuckles to himself and says, "Women, right? What can you do? This one's a real dingbat. Not two brain cells to rub together."

The air around the table turns heavy.

If my fingers weren't already locked into fists, they would be now. I feel my throat close, anger rushing in like heat under my skin. Carly's eyes dart between us, desperate to keep the peace, but there's no peace to be had.

Sam keeps smiling. Her fork trembles once before she steadies it. "So," she says brightly, "how's the sled hockey team doing?"

Murph picks up the cue instantly, his voice steady and cheerful. "We're short a few players, but morale's strong. Robbie's been killing it on defense."

"Yeah," Carly says quickly, jumping in. "He's gotten so fast lately, I can hardly believe it."

Sam seizes the lifeline. "I loved watching that practice. It was incredible."

Will looks bored. He reaches for his beer and drains half of it in one go. "You watch sports now?" he asks her flatly.

"I like supporting my friends," she says, her tone still light but her smile tighter.

He huffs. "Guess you've got more free time than I thought."

Silence spreads like a stain.

Murph clears his throat. "Who's up for dessert? Carly made pecan pie."

Everyone mutters some version of "sure." We eat quickly, no one saying much. Even Carly's careful conversation topics: travel plans, favorite shows, get swallowed up by Will's curt answers.

By the time we're done, I can feel my jaw aching from holding back every comment I want to make.

When Sam and Will finally stand to leave, Carly helps them with their coats. Sam gives me a quick, almost apologetic glance. "Thank you for inviting us," she says softly.

"Of course," I manage.

Will shakes Murph's hand or, more accurately, lets Murph shake his. "Good food," he says, already turning toward the door.

The door shuts behind them with a solid click.

The apartment stays quiet for a long time. The smell of roasted rosemary and gravy hangs in the air, suddenly too heavy.

I let out a long breath. "Pretty bad, huh?"

"Disgusting," Murph says immediately.

Carly bites her lip, still standing near the door. "You never really know what's going on in someone else's relationship, though, do you?" she says gently.

I look at her, stunned. "You're kidding, right?"

She shakes her head. "I'm not defending him. I'm just saying, Sam hasn't asked for help. We can't storm in and fix things she hasn't told us are broken."

"She's terrified," I say. "You saw her face."

Carly's eyes soften. She walks over and perches on the edge of Murph's seat where his lap would be, looping her arm around his shoulder. "I know, Rob. But you can't save someone who isn't ready to be saved. The best thing you can do is stay her friend. Be steady. Be safe."

It's the right advice, but it doesn't make it hurt any less. I nod, though my chest feels like it's caving in. "I just want her to be okay."

"I know," Carly says.

Murph gives me a look of quiet understanding, that silent, unspoken brotherhood that passes between men who know what helplessness feels like.

I take a slow breath, then turn toward the door. "If you'll excuse me, I'm heading home."

Carly jumps up and gives me a quick hug before I go. "You did good," she says. "You kept it together."

I don't answer, my throat is too tight.

The hallway outside Carly's apartment is quiet except for the faint hum of the elevator. I push the button with the side of my wrist and wait, staring at the floor. The patterned carpet blurs a little. My chest feels tight, like the tension of dinner is still sitting there, pressing down. By the time I get to my floor, the air feels too thick to breathe. I push into my apartment and roll to the window, shimming it open to get some fresh cold air.

I stare out at the parking lot below. The asphalt gleams under the streetlights, damp from the melting snow. I imagine Sam and Will walking to their car. I picture her doing what she always does, smiling like nothing's wrong, talking in that gentle way that smooths everything over. I wonder if he'll snap at her again once they're alone.

The thought makes something twist in my gut. I wish I could unsee it. The look on her face when he insulted her. The careful way she smiled through it, like she was apologizing for existing.

I tip my head back and exhale hard, but the sound that comes out isn't steady. It breaks in the middle.

It's not like me to cry. Not since the hospital, anyway. Not since the day they told me I'd never walk again and I realized the world I thought I knew had been bulldozed to rubble.

The tears start slow. One slips free, then another, and suddenly I can't stop. My shoulders shake, my chest heaves. It's ugly, quiet crying, the kind where you press your arm against your face and let it happen because there's no one here to hear you anyway.

The worst part isn't just that Will is cruel, it's how much I wish I could protect Sam from him, and how powerless I am to do it.

Samantha

In the car on the way home, the headlights wash over bare trees and frozen ground. The road hums beneath the tires, steady and hypnotic. I'm staring out the window, trying to lose myself in the rhythm of the drive when Will shakes his head, a short, sharp motion like he's flinging water off.

"What a pack of weirdos," he says, half laughing. "How do you even know them?"

His voice carries that mocking amusement I've come to dread, the kind that pretends to be light but has an edge of something else behind it.

I keep my eyes on the glass, watching the white lines streak by. "From the store," I say softly.

He lets out a laugh, dry and humorless. "Trust you to attract losers."

The words hit like a small stone to the chest. I'd been half-hoping that tonight might go differently. That maybe he'd see what I see in Robbie and Carly and Murph. That we could all sit together again one day, like normal friends. But Will doesn't really have friends. He has people he tolerates, and people he mocks.

I look out the window again, pretending I didn't hear. The cold reflection of my face in the glass looks steadier than I feel.

Over the next few days, he's in a better mood. Maybe my friends have become a new source of entertainment for him. "Pathetic losers," he says, chuckling over dinner. "Did you see the one guy with no legs? What the hell is wrong with this town?"

I give him the kind of smile that doesn't show teeth and say nothing. Whatever keeps him happy is okay with me.

But then Thursday comes.

I'm folding laundry when I hear his voice from the kitchen. "What is this?"

There's something in his tone that stops me mid-motion. A low, dark rumble. My body goes still before my mind even registers what's happening.

I walk carefully toward the kitchen, forcing my voice light. "What's that, sweetheart?"

He's standing by the counter, the open drawer of our mail and odds-and-ends pulled out. In his hand is the copy of *Pride and Prejudice*. Robbie's gift. The cover looks innocent, almost cheerful— pink and cream with soft lettering—completely out of place against Will's furious expression.

"Where did you get this?" His voice is calm in that terrifying way that means it won't stay calm for long.

My mind scrambles, flipping through possibilities, excuses, half-truths, but he's already seen my face. The blood drains from me and that's answer enough.

"It's just a gift from a friend," I say quickly. My voice barely comes out.

"A friend," he repeats, rolling the word like it's something foul. Then, faster than I can react, he hurls the book. It hits the wall beside my head with a loud, solid thud and falls to the floor. I flinch and that's all it takes. He sees it. He feeds on it.

"What friend?" he hisses, closing the distance between us.

"Just Robbie," I say before I can stop myself. I should have said Becca. I *should* have said anyone else. But panic scrambles logic, and the truth slips out like a confession.

His eyelid twitches. "Robbie? The crippled guy we had Thanksgiving with? That's who you've been seeing?"

"No...no," I stammer. "Just...he's nice. A friend. That's all."

"A friend who gives you gifts?"

"Books are nothing," I say, the words tumbling over themselves. "It's just...he lends me books sometimes. It's nothing."

Will's face twists into something hard and unreadable. He grabs my wrist suddenly, his grip sharp and unyielding.

"Will—"

He doesn't answer. He drags me toward the basement door, his fingers digging into my arm. The door rattles when he throws it open, and before I can process what's happening, he shoves me through.

My feet catch on the top step and I flail, grabbing the banister just in time. My shoulder jerks painfully, but I manage not to fall.

"Will!" I gasp.

The door slams. The lock turns.

The sound is small—just a quiet click—but it fills the whole room.

For a second, I don't breathe. My heart is hammering so fast it's almost a vibration. My hands shake. The air smells like dust and cold concrete.

"Will!" I call again, louder. No answer.

I press my palm to the door. "Please—"

Still nothing.

The silence that follows is worse than any shouting.

My knees go weak. I lower myself onto the step, forcing my breathing to slow, but every inhale shudders. My brain tries to reason its way out. Maybe he's cooling off, maybe he'll unlock the door in an hour.

He's never done anything like this before but it's not like it's that surprising of an escalation. He'll take some time to cool down and then we can talk it out.

The basement's dim, lit only by a thin line of light from the doorframe. The concrete floor stretches out below, cold and gray. There's a faint smell of laundry detergent from the washer and dust from the corners.

I focus on my breathing, counting the rhythm in my head until the trembling slows. If I let panic take over, I'll lose the small piece of control I have left.

"Just the here and now," I whisper to myself. "Don't think ahead."

I push my hair back and start scanning the room. There's an old storage trunk, a stack of boxes labeled *Christmas*, a folded camping chair, and the down blanket we haven't yet brought up for winter. I pull it around my shoulders, sinking onto the cold floor.

My pulse is still too fast. My wrist throbs where he grabbed me.

I try to think logically: he's angry, he'll cool down, he'll come back. This is punishment, not abandonment. I repeat that like a mantra, even as part of me wonders if I actually believe it.

After a while, the adrenaline drains out of me and exhaustion takes its place. I lie down on the blanket and close my eyes, the smell of dust filling my nose.

Somewhere above me, the pipes creak, the sound of the house breathing. It feels like the only proof that the world still exists beyond this door.

I wish I had the book. Something to hold, to focus on, to escape into.

But there's only the cold floor, the echo of my heartbeat, and the weight of my own silence.

So I pull the blanket tighter, curl in on myself, and wait for the sound of footsteps that might mean forgiveness.

Robbie

Samantha and I have a bit of a routine going. So when I come into the store the next day it's weird that I don't see her right away. Maybe she's helping someone else. I wait a few minutes by the entrance and then I start wheeling around the store but there's no sign of her. Eventually I see the store manager. She's a tall Indian woman named Tina.

She hustles over to me and says, "Do you know where Samantha is?"

Panic claws at my throat; I clamp it down. "I was going to ask you that," I say, keeping my voice steady, like I'm reading from a script.

Tina's brow creases. "She didn't show up for her shift and she didn't call, which is very unlike her." She looks hard at me, as if she's weighing whether I'm hiding the answer.

I try for a confident shrug. "Maybe she's sick. Maybe she forgot to call." My words sound thin even to my own ears.

A small woman has been listening: short, intense, eyes like she's cataloguing everything. She steps closer, almost into my personal space. "Are you talking about Sam?" she asks.

"Yes," I say cautiously. "Do you know something?"

"She was supposed to meet me here. Something is very wrong. She always keeps her promises."

"We shouldn't get too worried yet," Tina says. "I'm sure there's a perfectly mundane explanation and we're all going to laugh about this soon."

The other woman frowns, not believing a word of it. Customers drive grocery carts around us. Some of them shoot us dirty looks for taking up so much space but then they see I'm in a wheelchair and their faces contort to try not to feel annoyed.

"I'm Robbie," I say to the intense short woman. "I'm a friend of Sam's."

"Becca," she says. "Sam and I have known each other for sixteen years, five months, and..." Her eyes shift up to the side as she calculates, "ten days." The precision startles me. "So I know her very well and something is wrong."

The store's background noise, the beep of scanners, the squeak of a cart, swells in a way that makes the space feel too loud and too small.

Becca's stare softens fractionally. "She wouldn't miss shifts," she insists. "Something's wrong."

Tina, practical, rubs her temple and mutters she's going to call the store number again. "We'll keep looking," she says, then heads off with that manager's stride.

"Have you met her husband?" I ask, the question tumbling out because I'm thinking about the way he was treating her at our dinner.

Becca's mouth tightens. "I met him a few times. We don't get on." The words are flat, no flourish.

"I've only met him once but that doesn't surprise me," I say. "Do you think he's done something to her?"

"That does seem the most likely explanation to me."

"But how do we find out?"

She looks at me blankly and then shrugs. "Should I go over ot her house?"

"No," I blurt, the word sharp. "That could be dangerous." My mind races through scenarios: knock on the wrong door, tip Will off that someone is looking for her, make things worse. "I'll talk to my sister. Carly'll have ideas."

Becca flashes a look that says good, do that, and then fumbles her phone out. "Give me your number," she says. "I'll text you every update."

I list the digits and she instantly sends a text so I can save her to my contacts.

I push my chair out of the store with nothing more than an empty grocery list in the mesh under my seat and a growing hollow where routine used to be.

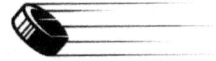

Instead of going to my apartment, I barrel through the halls straight to Carly's and pound on her door. No answer. Then I remember her laptop mornings and the Steamy Beans routine she sticks to like a metronome. Even though my shoulders are starting to ache from all the wheelchair pushing, I turn and roll in the direction of the café.

Steamy Beans smells of espresso and cinnamon when I push in. Carly is exactly where she always is: the window seat with her laptop open, a travel mug on the sill, sweater sleeves pushed up. She looks up, eyebrows knitting into the *are-you-serious* crease.

"Rob? Are you okay?" She's already halfway out of the chair before I say anything: instinctive, immediate.

"It's Sam. She's gone missing." My voice is thin and I can feel it wobble in a way I don't like. People glance. The owner, Kathleen, pauses mid-pour. A man at the counter raises an eyebrow, then looks away.

Carly drops her hands from the keyboard and gives me her full attention. "What do you mean?" she asks, practical and steady, the kind of focus that used to calm me down as a kid.

"She wasn't at work. She didn't call. Her phone's off." I spill the facts fast, as if speed will make them truer. "Tina checked. Becca's worried. I was at the store. We thought—" My words snag on the edge of *danger* and *what if*.

Carly frowns. "This doesn't sound like a hair-on-fire emergency," she says cautiously as though she's worried I'm about to roll off the deep end. She's probably right, honestly.

"What if he's murdered her?" That outburst attracts the attention of the people around us.

"Woah, woah, let's not jump to conclusions. No point borrowing trouble." She smiles tightly at the people around us as though to say, everything is fine here and please ignore the crazy man.

"I'm not." I press my palms into my wheels because I can't wring my hands. "She wouldn't miss work and not call. Her phone's off. Someone's got to check on her."

Carly exhales, eyes moving to the window as if the street outside might offer solutions. "Okay. First step: welfare check." She says it like a plan, methodical. "Call the non-emergency line. Ask the police to do a wellness check at her address. If they find her safe, we can breathe. If not—" Her voice tightens only a little. "We'll go from there."

"Yes," I say, relief and fear in the same breath. The plan gives me something to do that isn't panicking. I pull my phone out and use the speech to text to tell Becca that I'm contacting the police.

Samantha

He hasn't come back.

He hasn't let me out.

Time has stopped meaning anything down here. I don't know if it's been a day or two or three. The tiny rectangle of light under the door changes shade now and then, but it could be the bulb in the hall flickering for all I know. My throat feels raw from shouting. I've tried the door until my palms hurt: pounding, shaking the knob, pleadin— and still nothing.

At some point I stopped yelling. The silence that followed felt worse.

Now it's just me and the slow, steady sound of the house settling above me: the groan of pipes, the creak of old wood, the faint hum of the refrigerator that feels impossibly far away.

Hunger burns a hole through everything. My stomach twists and growls loud enough to echo. At first I try to ignore it but finally I start searching around for something, anything, down here to eat.

I find the jars in dusty rows on a low shelf behind a box of Christmas ornaments. The handwritten labels are smudged but legible: *Apple Pie Filling – 2022.* I can barely remember that version of me, the one who thought she could make a home from scratch, who spent hours in this very basement learning to can fruit to save a few dollars.

I twist one of the lids until my wrist aches, then finally pry it loose with the edge of a paint stirrer. The sweet smell hits me so hard it almost makes me cry. I dip my fingers into the thick syrup and taste it. It's cloying, sticky, too sweet to really enjoy, but it's food. It coats my tongue, my throat, and for the first time in hours the dizziness eases.

I eat half the jar before my stomach cramps from the sugar. I put the lid back on, careful, as if preserving it matters.

Then the quiet comes rushing back.

What is the plan here? Is Will waiting for me to starve? To beg? My thoughts turn darker the longer I sit. Maybe he doesn't have a plan. Maybe this *is* the plan, to let me waste away quietly where no one can see. My chest tightens as the thought takes shape.

He could get away with it. Easily. I have no family. He could say I left him, that I ran away. People would believe him; he's so good at performing. He always has been. He performed for me until we got married. I never saw a true thing about him until that day.

A shiver crawls over my skin despite the blanket I've wrapped around my shoulders.

I wanted more from my life. Not much, just *a little* more. A little peace. A little love. A little safety. Instead, I traded pieces of myself until there was nothing left but a shadow shaped to fit someone else's comfort.

All that time I thought I was helping him heal. That love could fix a broken man if I just poured enough of myself into him.

But you can't heal someone who doesn't want to change.

The thought comes like a slap.

And maybe this was always my fate. The words come unbidden— *fate, submission, atonement* — the old language of The Foundation still hiding in my bones like a virus. I thought I'd left it behind when I ran away all those years ago. But it's still here, whispering that I deserve this, that suffering earns redemption. That I should stay. That obedience is holy.

I press my hands to my ears as if I can block the thoughts out.

"I left," I whisper to the empty room. "I *left*."

But my voice sounds weak, unconvincing.

The air smells of apples and dust. My tongue is tacky with syrup. My stomach aches. My mind drifts to strange, hazy places, memories of The Foundation, of women kneeling to pray, of the leader's soft, lilting sermons about how endurance brings blessings. How pain purifies.

Maybe I've fought long enough. Maybe I was never meant to win. I thought I could make a new life, but all I've managed is a small job, a tiny home, an angry man. A string of days that start and end in fear.

My body feels heavy. My eyelids drift. I fade out for a while, lost somewhere between sleep and fainting, until a noise pulls me back.

A knock.

At first I think I've dreamed it, but then I hear it again, the distinct thud of a fist on wood. My heart leaps into my throat. I scramble upright, dizzy, clutching the railing as I drag myself up the steps. Each movement makes the wooden stairs groan.

I press my ear to the door.

Voices.

A man's—deep, steady—and then Will's, lighter, smoother, that laugh he uses when he's trying to charm someone. I can't make out the first words, but then the tone registers: official, polite, questioning.

A police officer.

They're asking about *me*.

My pulse hammers so hard I can feel it against the door. I strain to listen, pressing my cheek to the cold wood.

"...she's visiting her sister," Will says easily, and I can hear the smile in his voice. "Took a few days off work. You know how these things go. Someone probably misunderstood."

There's the muffled sound of agreement from the officer or maybe just politeness. Will laughs again, that deep, friendly sound that always fools people. He's good at this. So good that even now, part of me almost believes him.

I close my eyes and picture the scene: Will standing in the doorway, leaning casually on the frame, sleeves rolled up, wedding ring glinting. His voice warm, steady. The model husband. The officer nodding, reassured.

If I screamed right now, would he hear?

I imagine it: my voice clawing through the wood, echoing up the narrow hall, the officer pausing. Maybe he'd come closer. Maybe he'd break the door open. Maybe he'd believe me, maybe he wouldn't.

Or he wouldn't hear but Will would. He'd know I tried to call for help, get him in trouble, and the punishment would get worse.

My mind splits in two. One part of me is ready to throw myself against the door, to scream until my throat rips. The other part—the one shaped by years of obedience—whispers that I can't. That I *mustn't.* That a good wife endures. That this is a test of faith.

The words of my childhood murmur in my head like a chant: *The meek shall inherit the earth. A wife's duty is to bear her husband's burdens.*

Even now, when I don't believe any of it, I can't make my body move.

Tears sting my eyes.

I hear the door upstairs close. The voices fade. Silence again.

Missed my chance.

The sound that escapes me is half sob, half gasp. I sink back down the steps, trembling so hard I can barely grip the railing. My knees hit the concrete with a dull thud.

I'm so tired.

So hungry.

So *stupid,* just like he says.

I drag myself back to my nest: the folded blanket, the empty jar. The air is heavy, damp with my own breathing.

"It's over," I whisper, though the words catch on my dry throat. "It's over."

I've escaped before but not like this. A cult doesn't need to lock your door. They take away your options and fill you with fear about everything outside.

I pull the blanket over myself and curl up small, like if I make myself tiny enough the world might forget me.

Maybe this is how it ends: a quiet death in a dark basement, a woman who tried and failed to be good enough. A wasted little life. I hope at least the times I've made people smile in the grocery line made a difference in some way. I'm sorry I haven't been stronger.

But as my eyes close again, a small, fragile thought flickers in the back of my mind, a single spark against the dark:

If someone cared enough to send the police once, maybe they'll send them again. Maybe someone out there noticed my absence.

I hold onto that thought as I drift.

It's not hope exactly. Just the shadow of it.

Robbie

The police cruiser idles at the curb, headlights washing pale light across my chair. I can feel the vibration of the engine through the ground beneath my wheels. The officer leans against the hood, arms crossed, the picture of calm authority. He's looking down at me the way most people do when they're standing and I'm not: not intentionally cruel, just effortlessly condescending. .

"Samantha's fine," he says, as if repeating a nursery rhyme. I'm surprised he doesn't pat me on the head. "Her husband told us it was a last-minute family emergency, she went to visit her sister. She forgot to call, understandable in an emergency, right?" He taps his notepad once with a pencil, punctuating the story.

"But her phone is off," I say. The words feel small in the open air.

He gives a little shrug. "Probably lost charge. Happens all the time." Then, with that careful pitying look people get when they're about to dismiss you: "Listen, son, it's nice that you're looking out for her. But her husband mentioned you might be getting the wrong idea."

The words hang there. "Wrong idea?"

"Yeah," he says. "Your little crush is making her uncomfortable. The husband said it's been tough for her to figure out how to let you down easy. So he'd appreciate if you gave her a little space."

For a second, I can't find words. I stare up at him, my neck aching slightly from the angle, trying to process what he's saying. The wind cuts down the street, sharp and cold. Somewhere, a car door slams. The way he calls it a "little crush" lands like a slap. Like I'm a teenager with a puppy love fantasy, not a man who's spent months noticing small bruises on someone's arms and pretending they were nothing.

"Sir, that's not—"

He lifts a hand in the universal *that's enough* gesture. "It's over, son. We checked. She's fine. You can let it go now."

He's already turning away, keys jangling, the conversation done before it ever started.

The cruiser door shuts with a heavy click, the sound echoing off the quiet houses. I watch the taillights fade down the street until there's only darkness again.

Could it be true? Could I have misread everything?

My mind starts flipping through memories, rapid-fire: the way Sam smiled at me in the store, the light in her eyes when she talked about a book I brought her. Was I wrong about all of it? Were those just...kindnesses? The way she treats customers?

My chest tightens.

God, what if I've made her uncomfortable this whole time? What if she's been trying to tell me to back off and I just didn't get it?

The more I think about it, the more the doubt grows teeth. I picture her talking to Will, nervous, confessing that she has this disabled guy who keeps coming around, that she feels sorry for me, that she doesn't know how to make it stop. Will telling her she's too nice, too polite, and desperate people take it the wrong way.

The cop's tone, that careful, pitying cadence, suddenly makes sense. Maybe Will told him I was lonely, fragile. Maybe he said I'm obsessed. The idea makes my stomach twist.

Maybe I *am* wrong.

Maybe I've imagined it all.

By the time I roll away from the curb, the world feels tilted and wrong. I need someone else's take. Someone who knows Sam as more than a story told by her husband.

I pull my phone out and text *Becca* and *Carly*:

Meet me at Steamy Beans. Now. Urgent.

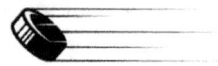

Becca's pacing when I roll up, her small frame cutting quick, nervous lines on the sidewalk in and out of the light of a streetlamp. Her hands flutter near her face as she spots me. "What happened? What did they say?"

"Let's go inside," I say, my voice rough from the cold.

Inside, the café hums with soft chatter and espresso steam. Carly's already there, her laptop bag at her feet, hands wrapped around a mug. She looks at me and something in her expression shifts; she sees that I'm more agitated, not less.

Becca sits on the edge of the couch, jittering. I park beside them.

"Okay," I start, the words thick. "The police went to check on Sam. Her husband told them she's visiting her sister. Last-minute family emergency."

Becca's head jerks up, eyes sharp as a blade. "That's an absolute lie," she says, standing so fast her knee bumps the coffee table. "Sam hasn't talked to her family in years. There's no sister visit. There's no contact."

I rub at the side of my neck. "That's not all he said." The words are hard to push out. "He told me Will said I've been bothering her. That she's uncomfortable." I hate how my voice breaks on the word. "I thought she liked talking to me, but...maybe I misread it. Maybe she was just being nice. God, what if I've been making her life worse?"

Both women freeze. Becca mid-fidget with the straw wrapper, Carly's hand paused over her coffee cup.

Carly's the first to move. She sets her mug down carefully, the ceramic clicking against the saucer, and leans forward. "Rob..." Her voice is quiet, steady, the kind she uses when she's talking someone off a ledge, usually me. "You didn't imagine this. We've seen her. Becca's seen the bruises. I've seen the way she flinches when his name comes up."

Becca nods vigorously. "And Sam doesn't fake kindness. That woman has been starving for safety, and you gave her a piece of it."

The words hit me hard enough that I have to look away. My throat tightens, my hands ache. The world outside the window blurs: headlights streaking past, rain starting to patter against the glass.

"But what if—" I start.

Carly cuts in, voice soft but firm. "If you'd crossed a line, she wouldn't keep showing up to talk to you. She wouldn't have invited you outside that day. She wouldn't have opened up about her past. You know the difference between compassion and obsession, Rob."

I sit there breathing hard, staring at the dark swirl of coffee on the table.

Becca's hand lands on my arm, quick and warm. "Will's the liar here. Don't let him gaslight you from two miles away."

I nod slowly. The fog of shame doesn't lift completely, but something steadier replaces it, the faint outline of anger, of purpose.

For a long moment, none of us speak. The smell of espresso drifts through the café, warm and bitter, grounding us.

"I'm going over there myself," Becca says suddenly. "If the cops won't do anything, I will."

"Becca, wait," Carly says, sharp but calm. "You can't. That's exactly what could get you—or her—hurt. You knock on that door and you'll confirm for him that people are watching. That could make things worse."

"What are we supposed to do? Sit here?" Becca snaps. Her hands tremble with adrenaline. "No one is doing *anything*."

Carly exhales slowly, then transforms from the worried friend into the analyst. "Okay. We do this smart. We call and request another welfare check but escalate it, tell them we have reason to believe there's domestic coercion, that previous checks may have been misled. We document everything: dates, times, who saw what. I'll look up domestic violence resources and the local victims' advocates. They'll know how to get an officer who won't accept the husband's story at face value."

Becca has her notebook out. "I can make a timeline," she says.

"I have hockey practice," I say finally, the weight of responsibility pressing against the urgency. "And then I have to work." My voice is small. The day's events press like a wet coat on my shoulders. "But I'm not giving up."

Carly reaches over and squeezes my shoulder. "We'll be ready when you get out. Call us the second you hear anything." Her hand is steady, rooted. "You did the right thing calling it in. Don't let that cop make you doubt yourself."

I nod, swallowing hard. "I just...want her safe."

"You care," Carly says. "That's not a crime."

I nod but don't say anything else, just head out into the rain.

"You okay there, Rob?" Murph asks.

"Yeah." I try to make the word sound normal and end up slamming my stick so hard the puck rockets off the wall with a wet *smack*. The sound fills the rink. I grab another and do the same. I've got this urge to keep smashing things until the racket drowns whatever's in my head, but the truth is my arms don't have the power to actually break anything anymore. The effort leaves them burning and me deflated, like a balloon with a tiny hole. I drop my stick onto the ice and the noise of it clinking dies out. I let out a long, useless sigh.

Murph watches me the way he watches everything: patient, steady. He has that calm about him, the kind that makes you want to shove words into the silence just so the quiet doesn't look like weakness. What I'm trying not to think keeps thudding against the inside of my skull like someone pounding on a door.

"Sam is missing," I say finally. The sentence comes out flat. "And I think her husband did something to her." I smack another puck as hard as I can, the stick vibration running up my forearms. "I want to run into that house and brash his fucking brains in. I want to carry Samantha out in my arms and protect her." I want to be who I was before and not know the first fucking thing about spinal cord injuries.

Even though I didn't say that last part out loud, Murph knows. Every disabled person knows.

He doesn't chastise me. He doesn't soft-coach me. He just says, "Don't drive yourself mad with what-ifs. If you didn't get injured, you wouldn't even be in Cedar Harbor to meet Sam. There's no way of untangling the threads that pull us through life. In the here and now, as we are, we are going to help her." Again I see the shadow of the soldier in him who will always protect and serve.

"We are?"

Murph nods and, with that quiet command he has, whistles low. "Danny. Mark." He flicks his eyes toward the bench.

They come over to where we are. Danny is fast, quick at propelling with the sticks. Mark is much slower, still learning to move the sled. He looks younger than I expected up close eager..

"We have an issue," Murph tells them, voice clipped into business. "Robbie's friend, Samantha, is in trouble and no one seems to be doing anything about it."

Mark's brow tips up. "What kind of trouble?"

I answer before Murph can. "Her sleazebag husband is hiding her or something." The words come out harsher than I mean to, a hard little stone thrown across cold water.

"At this point," Murph says levelly, "we don't even know if she's alive."

I think I'm going to be sick.

Murph doesn't let the fear settle in. "First step: survey the house. Confirm whether she's there. Second step is keep track of his schedule. We find times when he's out. Third step: we'll figure ingress and egress. If there's a back door, windows, a path, we find it. If we can't confirm she's there, steps two and three are still necessary. Either we go in to help her escape or we go in to find clues to her whereabouts."

Surveillance sounds so cinematic in my head. In practice, it's awkward. How do you hide four guys in wheelchairs without looking like a rolling stakeout? On the other hand, people tend to underestimate us. Maybe that will work to our advantage.

Danny sees the blank look on my face and slaps his thigh like a rallying cry. "She needs us and we're not letting disability get in the way of that. We're the goddamn wheelchair mafia and we're coming for him." He says it with a grin wide and ridiculous enough that I have to laugh. It is ridiculous...and exactly what we need.

Something like hope flickers in my chest. I'm not alone. We're the wheelchair mafia and we're fighting back.

Murph pulls out his phone and asks for Sam's address. Becca had texted it earlier; I pass it over. Murph taps the screen and pulls up Street View. The four of us cluster around the phone, breath fogging in a little cloud of urgency.

"This is the front of the house," he says, pointing at the screen. The picture is a classic New England cottage: clapboard siding, a steep roof, a porch with posts, a small stoop. "Obviously not accessible," he notes. The driveway looks narrow. "Can't see the back. Assume no wheelchair access there either."

Mark leans in, practically vibrating. He's thrilled to be part of something that matters. "I'll be the point person," he says. "I'll keep notes. I can observe the house after school." His voice is all nerves and resolve.

"Danny," Murph continues, "you can pretend you're doing work in the area. You know, contractor stuff. Check the layout, get close enough to take photos without looking suspicious. Send observations to Mark. Time-stamp everything."

Danny nods. "I can swing by with a pickup or a clipboard. Act like I'm measuring for a fence. No one bats an eye."

I choke out a quiet, "Thank you."

Murph claps a hand on my shoulder, big and solid. "Wheelchair mafia... I like it," he says with a crooked grin. "Now go home, try not to worry, and get to your shift. We'll take it from here." He squeezes my shoulder before he releases me.

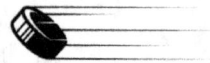

By the time I get to my car, my arms are trembling from more than effort. The adrenaline that's been keeping me upright is starting to burn off, leaving nothing but exhaustion and nerves. I pull myself into the driver's seat, break down my chair, stow it in the passenger seat, and sit there for a minute with my forehead pressed against the steering wheel.

Go home. Work your shift. Don't worry. Sure, Murph. Easy to say for someone whose heart isn't currently trying to punch through their ribcage.

When I finally make it back to my apartment, the blue light from my computer screen cuts a sharp line through the dark. I go through the motions: logging in, opening the customer service portal...but my brain refuses to cooperate.

"Thank you for calling SilverLine Shipping," I say automatically as the first customer connects. "How can I help you track your package today?"

The woman on the other end talks about a missing box of tea candles. I try to sound calm, to keep my voice warm and practiced, but my mouth twitches restlessly. Half my attention is on the call, the other half on Sam. Where she might be, whether she's still alive, whether Will has realized people are looking for her.

The customer thanks me. I disconnect. Another call pops in before I can even take a breath.

Same script. Same hollow rhythm. I check my phone every few minutes, even though I know I'll see the screen light up if Murph texts.

By the third call, I can't remember what anyone's ordered. I'm nodding and smiling into the headset, hearing myself say all the right things, but my stomach's in knots. Every time there's a noise in the hallway outside my apartment: a door closing, a set of footsteps, I flinch.

When my silent timer buzzes, I go through the routine of pressure relief, pushing up on my fists to shift my weight. The motion burns in my shoulders, but it's almost a relief to have something physical to do. Something I *can* control.

The next customer complains about a late delivery, but her voice fades into static. My mind drifts again to an image of Sam smiling one day at the grocery store, her hair falling into her face as she tucked it behind her ear. To the way she said, *You make the day go faster.*

I rub my wrists over my face and force myself to focus on the screen. One hour left in the shift. One hour until I can call Murph and find out if they've learned anything. Then I'll have to go to bed. I'm useless to Sam if I don't get sleep.

Samantha

The tiniest window sits high on the basement wall, a slit of dusty glass no bigger than a shoe box. Most of the time it feels like it's mocking me. But it lets in light, and that light has become my only clock.

Each day I've watched the sun shift, trying to measure time in slices of gold and gray. The light in the morning is thin, silver-pale; by afternoon it burns warmer, then fades again to the color of bone. I think I've been here four days. Maybe five. I've stopped being sure.

Today, when the light is at its strongest, I'm staring up at the window again when something moves.

At first it's just a shadow that passes, quick and strange. Then another. I squint and my pulse starts to race.

A shape fills the frame: the rubber edge of a tire, a scuffed sneaker, a metal footplate pressed against the glass.

My breath catches.

That can't be—

I scramble up and stretch on shaking legs to pound my hand against the window. Dust falls down around me. "Hello?" My voice is hoarse, barely audible even to me. I reach up and tap, then tap again, praying whoever it is hasn't gone.

There's a pause. Then, from the other side, a knock answers mine. Soft but deliberate.

I press my palm to the cold glass. A heartbeat later, knuckles touch the other side, just enough to make contact.

Robbie.

I'd know those unique fingers anywhere.

He probably can't lean far enough for me to see his face, but I can picture it: brow furrowed, focused, determined. He's here. He's found me. Or at least, he's *trying* to.

My knees buckle. I sink to the floor, tears blurring the light that leaks through.

He knows something's wrong. He *cares.*

I don't have words for what that realization does to me. It's not just relief, it's something deeper, almost cellular, like a switch being flipped back on after years of darkness.

For so long I've been shrinking, trying to make myself small enough not to upset Will, quiet enough to survive.

But Robbie being out there makes me feel something I haven't in years: worth. It's not that I want to trade one man for another. It's about more than him specifically, it's what his presence represents. Proof that goodness exists, that not every man uses strength to dominate. Robbie's kindness, his persistence, his refusal to look away...those things mean I can stop believing this is the only life I deserve.

My reflection shimmers faintly in the glass as I whisper, "Thank you."

He can't hear me. He doesn't need to.

I will survive this. I can start over. I've done it before.

I remember the night I left my home. How my heart pounded so hard I thought it would give me away. I'd slipped out barefoot with my shoes in my hand, still wearing the only kind of clothes I had: an ankle-length skirt and long-sleeved blouse. I didn't know what waited for me in the world beyond those gates, but I went anyway. Because I knew if I stayed, I would vanish.

That girl—that terrified, stubborn, desperate girl—is still inside me. Will didn't kill her. He just buried her under years of manipulation and fear. How did I forget that?

How did I let him wear me down so completely that I stopped believing I was capable of saving myself?

Back then I spent a few nights on the street, sleeping in a bus terminal, until I found out about shelters. From then on I walked all day and slept in shelters at night until I found Becca. Almost everyone has at least one person on the outside who can help them when they leave a cult. I didn't have much to go on, I didn't have a phone number. But I found her and lived with her family for the next several years.

My sweet, awkward, brilliant Becca. The idea of her never explaining another joke to me makes my chest ache. There are people out there who miss me.

The window glows brighter for a moment, Robbie's chair shifting, a small movement that tells me he's still there. Maybe he's talking to someone. Maybe he's figuring out what to do next.

I press both palms to the glass. The cold burns, but it feels like a promise.

There are people who want me to live. I whisper it to the empty air, the walls, the cold floor: "I choose life."

The words feel fragile at first, then stronger. I say them again, louder this time.

"I choose life."

The echo bounces down into the basement, and something inside me steadies.

Now I just have to figure out *how*.

I turn from the window and look around with new eyes: not like a trapped woman waiting to die, but like someone planning her next move. There's the shelving unit, the old storage trunk, a broom handle. Tools. Options.

If I could pry the hinges, loosen a vent, send a message through the pipes...It doesn't matter yet how.

What matters is that I've decided.

I'm not going to die down here. I will not stay quiet. I will not be obedient. I will not shrink myself until I disappear.

Robbie

Hockey practice has been completely abandoned in favor of wheelchair mafia planning sessions.

"Now I know he's keeping her in the basement," I say. "Is that enough to go to the police with? Can they do something?" I look around me but the guys' faces are not hopeful.

"None of us are in that profession," Danny says. "We don't really know."

Mark fidgets with the joystick on his power chair and looks apologetic. "I watch a lot of crime shows and I don't think finding her by peeking in a window would hold up."

"I have to go in there and get her," I blurt. Of course I know how stupid that sounds. I don't even know how I'm going to get up the front stairs. I want to be the man who charges into that house and grab Sam from that monster. I just can't figure out how I'm going to do it.

"Robbie, listen," Murph says, steady and blunt. "If I let you put yourself in harm's way, Carly would never forgive me."

"If it was her who was kidnapped, what would you do?" My voice is sharper than I mean. I can see the cloud of anger pass across his face at the thought of Carly being held and him doing nothing about it.

Murph's jaw tightens. Silence stretches, and then he exhales. "Okay. Let's figure this out."

The room snaps into action like a well-practiced play. Danny suggests plywood for a ramp. It's not ideal but it's quick. "We can make a run for the porch," he says. Mark, eyes bright with a dangerous kind of excitement, volunteers to be the battering ram. "I can bash the door open with my chair," he says, almost giddy at the thought.

I wonder if there have been any court cases where a wheelchair was ruled a weapon. Mark's chair is heavy enough he could probably run over Will's feet and at least incapacitate him.

Murph's expression goes grim but determined. "We're going to pick a time when Will's out now that we have his schedule. If the battering ram idea fails, who can pick a lock?"

Danny pipes up. "I can pick simple locks."

The sound of the plan getting inked into reality is oddly soothing.

"This is the dumbest thing I've ever been involved in," Murph says, then tilts his head and grins. "But let's give it a try."

"Hell yeah," I say, pounding a fist into my thigh. No more waiting, now we act and we act quick to get her out of there. "Do I need a gun?" I ask, suddenly. I've never held one.

"Absolutely not," Murph says instantly, giving me a look that says he knows exactly how badly handing me a gun would go.

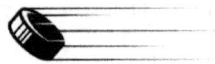

The plan is in motion at last.

Danny and I ride shotgun in Murph's car, the heater blasting and all three of us silent, listening to the rhythmic slap of windshield wipers. The weight of what we're about to do hums between us like static. The smell of old coffee clings to the upholstery.

We don't have a vehicle that would accommodate Mark's power chair and we couldn't exactly ask his mother to drop him off for breaking and entering but he has a part-time caretaker who he talked into bringing him.

By the time we all meet in front of Sam's house, dusk is sinking into night. The street is quiet. Will's car isn't in the driveway, exactly as planned. He's supposed to be at his AA meeting until nine.

Danny pulls the plywood plank from the back of the car. The board looks flimsy, warped from an old job, and there's no way it could support the weight of Mark's chair. I see the disappointment in Mark's face when Murph confirms it with a shake of his head. His fingers twitch on his joystick, eager for action.

"Sorry, maybe next time," he says with a wry smile, as though we're going to start making a habit of this.

The house looms in front of us, a squat New England cottage, white paint gone dull gray, the porch light burned out. There's a stillness about it that makes the hair on my neck stand up.

Danny positions himself in front of the stairs, grabs the railing with one hand, and hauls himself upright. His leg muscles tremble with the effort, but he's determined. We all watch, holding our breath, as he painstakingly pulls himself up each step and strains to reach the doorknob while still holding onto the railing with his other hand. "Locked," he calls back, "but not deadbolted."

A good sign. My pulse kicks up.

Murph and I angle the plywood against the steps while Mark steadies the bottom edge with his chair. Murph's biceps flex as he shoves Danny's empty wheelchair up to the porch. It rattles onto the porch. Danny lowers himself into it, breathing hard, and digs a small toolkit from his jacket pocket.

"Picked worse locks than this," he mutters, biting the edge of his lip as he works. The rest of us wait on the lawn, the night air thick with nerves. Every crunch of gravel under my tires sounds like a gunshot. I glance down the street, heart thudding, half-expecting headlights to appear. Sam's house is isolated, though, and I don't think any neighbors can see us through the thick pine trees. In the quiet I can hear Danny's tiny, focused movements: a click, a scrape, another click. Then—

"Got it!" The door swings open with a low creak.

I feel a chill roll through me. It's not cold—not really—but the darkness inside that doorway feels heavy, like stepping into a cave. My throat goes dry.

But Sam is in there. And I am not leaving without her.

"Push me up," I say.

"Okay," Murph says, his voice betraying a hint of hesitation. He sees me as Carly's kid brother and I know he wants to protect me but he also knows I'm all in on this and the best he can do is mitigate the risk.

Danny holds the board steady from above, Mark braces the bottom corner with one wheel. Murph plants himself behind me at the bottom of the ramp, sets his brakes, and presses his palms to the back of my chair. "Ready?"

I grip my rims the best I can and Murph gives me a strong push to get started. Slowly I eek my way up. My arms scream with effort, my chest tightens from the strain, but I don't stop. The last shove gets me over the lip of the makeshift ramp, and I roll forward into the open door.

"You good, Rob?" Danny calls from the porch. "I'm going to go around back and try to get better cell signal."

"Yeah, sounds good, man," I say without looking back. Everything inside is still and silent. The foyer is narrow, wallpaper curling in corners, shadows pooling where the light doesn't reach. It's hard to believe anyone is here but I saw Sam's hand pressed on the glass of the basement window.

I move slow, scanning for the basement. The first door I try opens into a pantry. My gut twists. I can't tell if it's adrenaline or nausea. I keep going. Down the hall, I see another door: chain lock at the top, a standard lock below. My pulse spikes.

I knock softly. "Sam? Are you there?"

For a few seconds, silence. Then I hear movement, quick, uneven, and a soft, broken whisper. "Robbie? Is that you?"

The relief nearly knocks me out of my chair. "Sure is," I say, forcing my voice steady. "Hold tight, I'm getting you out."

Turning the lock in the doorknob is simple enough when I use both hands but the chain is another matter. It's pretty high up but luckily I do have long arms. I get close to the door, press my right fist against it and start sliding my arm up braced against the door until I can feel the edge of the metal lock. I strain as tall as I can in my wheelchair, pressing down with my other fist on the seat to lift me up more, and get my knuckles around the bolt. It takes all my strength but the chain slips free with a sharp *clink*.

I slump forward, panting. "You're good," I say. "Come out."

The door creaks open, and there she is: Sam. Her face is pale, her eyes wide and sunken, but alive. She steps into the hallway like she's afraid the floor will swallow her.

"Hey," I whisper. "You're safe now."

She starts to speak, but a voice cuts through the air behind me. "Well, look at this."

The hairs on my arms rise. I turn.

Will stands at the top of the stairwell to the second floor: broad, smirking, hands shoved into his pockets. His eyes gleam in the dim light. "Look at you," he says slowly, stepping down each stair with deliberate control. "Trying to save the day."

My blood goes cold. The sound of his boots against the steps feels like a countdown.

"I knew something was off," he says, "you snooping little freaks watching my house." His voice drips amusement, but there's danger underneath, that low rumble before a storm hits.

He keeps coming. Sam presses herself behind me, her breath trembling. I can feel the fear coming off her like heat. I roll forward, my chair's wheels squeaking against the wood floor.

I glance behind him to the open door, catch Murph's eye. But Will notices and turns to see Murph preparing to try to rush up the ramp and he slams the front door shut and locks it. Turning back, he tilts his head.

"Are you really a cripple?" he asks, almost incredulous. Like someone is pranking him.

If ever there were a time to miraculously stand up and be able to physically attack him, now would be it. But that's not going to happen. This might be the end of me but I will admit at least to myself that I love Sam and I'm going to do absolutely everything I can to protect her no matter what it costs me.

"Yes," I say evenly.

Will shakes his head and laughs. "Delusional," he mutters. "Absolutely deranged."

I don't actually stand a chance but hopefully the other guys have called the police by now. I just hope they get here before Will beats me to a pulp or literally kills me.

Samantha

I can feel the weight of every moment of my life pressing into this one heartbeat. The basement. The cult. The wedding vows. The years of silence. Every tiny compromise I made to survive: they all led here, to this single point where everything either changes or ends.

Robbie is in danger because of *me*. He's sitting there in his wheelchair, chest heaving, completely exposed to Will's rage. And Will...Will is smiling. That slow, wolfish smile that means he's going to hurt someone.

I know how this ends if I do nothing. We're both going to die.

The air hums with tension. The two men's words blur into noise while my heartbeat pounds in my ears. My hands tremble, but my mind is suddenly clear.

I've been brave once before.

When I ran away from The Foundation, it was to save myself. Now I have to be brave again, this time to save someone else.

I scan the room, desperate for something, *anything* I can use, but there's nothing. Just walls, shadows, a man's heavy boots planted inches from me. I think of things I've seen in movies and I can only hope they work in real life too.

Slowly I start inching around the confrontation, trying not to be noticed so I can get into position. I want to hurry, afraid that Will is going to punch Robbie to the floor at any moment, but if I move fast I'll attract attention. I need them to stay focused on each other for just a few more minutes.

I breathe in shallow, steady gulps. Every sound becomes too loud: the scrape of Will's boots on the floor, Robbie's breathing, the tick of the clock on the mantle. My hands are slick with sweat even though the room is cold.

I move in fractions, the kind of small, careful shifts I learned as a server, how to stand behind someone's blind spot without being noticed. My feet barely make a whisper against the wood. I keep my head low and my shoulders loose so I don't make the hard, defensive shapes that invite notice.

Will's face is inches from Robbie's. He's leaning in, the predator's posture, all authority and cruel amusement. His voice is a low hum in my ears, centred on taunting.

I slide along the shadowed wall, fingers grazing the wallpaper to keep my balance, every muscle tuned to silence. The hallway seems to narrow and lengthen at once; time stutters between heartbeats. Even my breath feels too loud and my heart hammering so hard that he must surely hear me but no, Will's focus is completely on the sick pleasure he gets from humiliating another man. He loves lording it over others when he's winning at something and right now he's sure he's going to win this. After all, how could he not?

I take one more, careful step. The floorboard under my left foot gives a tiny complaint; I freeze until Will's laugh, mean and bright, fills the space and smooths the sound into ordinary noise. The miracle of it, that something so ordinary can be a mask for monstrous things, makes bile rise in my throat.

I move again. My heart is a drum but my hands are steady now, focused on a single point in my mind: hold on, don't let go, don't let him hurt Robbie.

I launch myself onto Will's back, my fingers locking around each other across his throat. The impact knocks the air out of me, but I hold tight, pulling back with every ounce of weight I have.

He bellows, surprised and furious, stumbling backward into the wall. The sound rattles the picture frames. My teeth grind as he thrashes, elbows striking at my ribs, but I don't let go.

"Get off me!" he snarls, his voice cracking with effort. His skin is slick under my palms, muscles straining against me.

I think of the cult leader's face when he accused me of stealing, of all the times I was told to stay quiet, to submit. I think of Will's laughter when he locked me in the basement, his words echoing down the stairs.

And I pull harder.

My entire world shrinks to the place where my hands meet at his throat: the burn of friction, the ragged sound of his breath, the scream in my shoulders. Every ounce of fear in me ignites into fury.

He lurches, tries to throw me off, and I hold tighter, teeth gritted, a low growl tearing from my throat. He's strong, but I'm desperate.

The room tilts, furniture blurs, the sound of his choking fills my head like thunder.

Then, finally his fight starts to weaken. His movements slow, grow jerky, his hands clawing at mine.

"Sam," he croaks, barely audible.

I don't loosen. Not yet. I count my breaths—one, two, three—and when I hear the rasp turn to a wheeze, I release.

Will collapses forward, hitting the floor hard. His body heaves once, twice, then goes still except for the faint rise and fall of breath.

I tumble beside him, my palms burning, lungs on fire. For a second I can't tell if the world is spinning or if I am.

"Sam?" Robbie's voice. Breathless, close. I turn my head and see his chair angled toward me, his hand reaching out, fingers curled but steady. I grab it, pressing his fist against my palm like an anchor.

And then I hear it: the distant cry of sirens, faint but growing louder, closer.

"Are you okay?" Robbie asks, his eyes wide and wet with fear.

"Yes," I whisper. "Are you?"

He nods, a shaky smile flickering through his fear. "I am...thanks to you."

For years I've been told I'm weak, useless, stupid. But here, now, today, I did it. *I saved us.*

There's a knock at the door. Sharp, commanding. "Police! Open up!"

Robbie exhales, relief washing over his face. "Thank God."

I stagger to my feet on trembling legs and make my way to the door. The handle feels cold, grounding. When I open it, bright light floods the room. The officers are there, voices clear and professional, and behind them on my lawn are the entire sled hockey team. Murph, Danny, and Mark, all lined up like a strange little army. Their faces are drawn tight with worry, but when Robbie waves through the window, they all sag with visible relief.

The police step inside, scanning the scene: me, shaking and tear-streaked, Robbie in his chair, Will unconscious on the floor. One officer gently takes my elbow and guides me to the couch. His voice is kind but blurred at the edges.

"Ma'am, can you tell us what happened?"

I start to explain...the basement, the door, the chain, Robbie's courage...but my voice catches when I see him out of the corner of my eye. He's watching me, eyes glassy with exhaustion and something deeper. Pride, maybe.

And for the first time in years, I feel something rise in me that isn't fear. It's fragile and radiant, like sunlight breaking through water.

By the time Will stirs, there are handcuffs on his wrists. He groans, confused, blinking up at the officers as they pull him to his feet. His gaze locks on mine, desperate, pleading.

"Samantha," he rasps. "Tell them it's a misunderstanding."

Once, that voice would have undone me. Once, I would have apologized for making him angry.

But now Robbie's hand rests lightly on my leg, a quiet, solid reminder that I don't have to go back.

I say nothing. Will's face twists in confusion as they lead him out into the night.

The moment the door shuts behind him, I deflate and sink my head into my hands.

It's over. The whole nightmare is over.

I don't know what comes next. The questions swarm: legal, practical...terrifying.

Will my husband stay in jail? Will his mother bail him out? Am I safe in my home? What does my future look like now? How do I file for divorce? Do I need money for a lawyer? The overwhelm of all these questions is one of the reasons I never tried to change my situation before.

Tomorrow. Tomorrow I'll think about all that. Tonight I will just feel relief that it's over and pride that I stood up for myself at last.

Robbie

I didn't tell my sister ahead of time that I was confronting Sam's husband. I knew if I had, she would have stopped me. But now that it's over and everyone's intact (or at least as intact as we were before), I finally call her.

The phone rings twice.

"What's going on?" Carly says the moment she answers. She never says hello; she just cuts straight to suspicion. I almost never call, so her guard's already up.

"Sam's husband just got arrested."

There's a sharp intake of breath. "Oh my God! What happened? Are you okay?"

"I'm fine," I say. My voice sounds steadier than I feel. My muscles are still humming with leftover adrenaline. "She needs a safe place to stay. Do you know where she can go?"

That's my sister's language: logistics, plans, problem-solving. It's how she copes when things get too big to feel. But she isn't distracted into planning as she usually would be. Instead of answering right away, she says, "Did you have anything to do with this?"

The silence that follows is my answer.

"Wait," she says slowly. "Did Kevin help you with this?"

Now we're both in trouble. Carly's going to kill me and Murph might not escape unscathed either. But I'll take her protective anger over letting Will keep hurting Sam any day.

"Do you know a place or not?" I ask.

Carly sighs. I can picture her pinching the bridge of her nose. "Okay, okay. Yes. I'll come pick her up. Give me the address."

I rattle it off. "Be careful," I add.

She huffs. "That's my line."

I smile and instruct my phone to hang up. The silence that follows feels huge, the kind that fills every corner of a room when the chaos finally stops.

I roll over to Sam, who's sitting on the couch, wrapped in a blanket one of the officers found. Her hair's tangled, her face blotchy from crying, but she's beautiful in a way that makes my chest ache.

"Carly's on her way," I tell her. "She'll find you somewhere safe to stay, okay?"

Sam nods, her hands twisting in her lap. "You...you really thought I was worth all this?"

"Of course," I say simply.

She smiles, small, shy, but real. "Thank you for not giving up on me."

"Never." I know now without a doubt that I love her but it's not the time to tell her that. She's dealing with a lot and she has healing to do. It's enough for me to know that I love her and I will do everything in my power to see her happy.

"I can't believe you got everyone working to help me," she says after a moment. "You really had a whole team out there."

"Wheelchair mafia, baby." I grin. "We don't mess around."

Her smile widens. "I guess I owe my life to the wheelchair mafia."

"Don't worry," I say. "We'll bill you later."

That earns me a soft laugh and for the first time, she looks like herself again.

Outside, headlights wash across the windows. Carly's car pulls up. The police are still milling around, finishing their reports, but the energy has shifted. The danger is gone. What's left is the messy work of beginning again.

Boots crunch on gravel outside, and through the door I hear my sister say to Murph, "I'll be talking to you later."

Murph mutters something in return, probably an apology wrapped in humor, but Carly doesn't answer. Her footsteps are fast and certain on the porch. Then she's framed in the doorway, hair wild around her cheeks, eyes red and furious.

She doesn't say a word. She just crosses the room in three strides and folds herself around me. The force of it almost knocks the air out of my lungs. For a second, I just sink into the smell of her: coffee and winter and that floral shampoo she's used since college.

"Hey, hey, I'm okay," I mumble into her shoulder, though my voice cracks halfway through. My hands hover uselessly before I manage to tap the back of her arm.

"You idiot," she whispers into my hair, her voice breaking at the end. She squeezes tighter before finally pulling back, her eyes shining with tears she refuses to let fall.

For a heartbeat, we just look at each other. She brushes her thumb under her eye like she's brushing away dust.

Then she turns toward Sam. Her whole posture shifts, the anger smoothing into something gentler. "Come on," she says softly, her voice the kind she used when we were kids and I'd gotten hurt. "Let's get you somewhere warm."

Sam hesitates, her fingers twisting in the edge of the blanket around her. The room feels fragile, like if any of us speak too loudly, the quiet calm will shatter.

Carly waits, patient, steady as ever, holding out her hand. Slowly, Sam nods and takes it.

"I'll see you soon?" Sam asks me.

"Count on it," I say.

She walks out between Carly and an officer, her shoulders hunched but her steps steady. When I see her get into Carly's car and close the door, I let out the breath I've been holding for what feels like hours.

From the lawn at the bottom of the plank of plywood, Murph calls up, "You need help getting down?"

"Uh, just hold it steady?"

Murph angles himself at the bottom, leaving the end of the ramp clear but the corner stoppered by his wheel. I push out the door and careen down the old wood completely out of control. Despite that, I land safely at the bottom, still upright.

Murph slaps the hood of his car twice. "Let's go home, hero."

"Don't start," I say, but my mouth twitches.

We both get in. The tires crunch over gravel, carrying us away from that house. The flashing lights fade behind us until there's only the dark, the hum of the road, and the low rumble of Murph's car.

I lean my head against the cold window and let my eyes drift shut.

The End

Thank you for reading! If you enjoyed this book I hope that you'll consider **leaving a review** wherever you purchased this book and/or Goodreads. It helps a lot :)

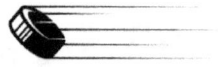

You can get **bonus scenes,** short stories, character art, and more at my website: https://ruthmadisonbooks.com/bo nusincluding spicy scenes for all Cedar Harbor titles and "Wheelchair Mafia" merch.

Becca

Am I a bad person? What is bad or good when it comes to being a person anyway? My parents always told me there are no bad people, just bad actions and my observations so far have borne that out. I've never seen any bad behavior that I couldn't follow the thread back to fear. Scared people do scary things. But are they bad?

That's what I'm wondering as a gossip video plays on my TV and I knit a lace shawl for my sister's wedding veil. I wonder why I enjoy these videos gossiping about reality shows and does that enjoyment make me a bad person. My knitting needles continue to clack away as my mind goes deeper and deeper into this question. Luckily I have the lace pattern memorized by now.

I'm not convinced that Leah actually wants me at her wedding but it would look strange if her own sister wasn't there so we have to do what's expected. Life would be nicer without the weight of those expectations. What if it were fine to admit that she doesn't particularly like me and not have it be a big deal?

I also don't think I'll enjoy the wedding much. I've never been to one but I understand there's a lot of people, loud music, crowded spaces, talking to people you don't know, and trying to look entertained by speeches. I shudder just thinking about it. Leah's going to make me be a bridesmaid too. Probably even maid of honor. She'll never agree to noise-cancelling headphones so I'll have to wear earplugs and style my hair to cover them.

A funny commercial comes on the TV and I carefully lay down the knitting to pick up my notebook and write down the joke. I appreciate the juxtaposition of a serious person of power and authority doing something silly and mundane. Unexpected pairings like that can make great humor.

My phone alarm buzzes and it's nearly time for me to go over to my volunteer job at Thatcher memorial rehab center. I've given myself enough buffer that I have time to finish the row of knitting and fold it into my basket. Then I brush my thick wavy brown hair because my mother has told me never to leave the house without brushing it first. And even though I now live in an apartment and not a house, I do it anyway. I believe the intention of her statement was that no one outside see my hair in an unruly state. Brushing does not always accomplish that goal, however.

With my hair properly frizzed, I pick out a pair of my favorite socks. Once I found these socks I bought enough of them to get rid of all my other socks. The difference between these socks and the ones I used to have is subtle but when your senses don't process input correctly the right clothes help a lot. What I've learned over the years is that if I can do small things to avoid irritation it greatly reduces the chance of me having a meltdown. The little challenges and sensory processing issues build up until they reach explosion so if I can bring the stress levels back down in any way it prolongs the period of time I can spend out doing people things.

In my bag I have a light cardigan in case the air on my arms starts to bother me, ear plugs, a smooth stone that feels nice to stroke, a bottle of water and a snack bar. Before I leave my apartment I make sure it's all still packed in my bag and then I drive over to Thatcher.

I work from home so this volunteer job is one of the only things that gets me out of the house regularly, which is good for me. So my mother says.

Thatcher is a rehabilitation facility mostly for people with spinal cord injuries but they have patients learning to use wheelchairs for other reasons too.

I feel a kinship with the patients here even though I'm disabled in a very different way. However, I rarely talk to anyone. My job is to restock shelves, move chairs in and out of meeting rooms, fix little things. The staff do sometimes ask for my help with their computers because they know I work as a coder.

Just because I don't speak much doesn't mean I'm not listening so I hear all the gossip and drama about staff and about patients. Today one of the nurses is leaning over the reception desk and talking about a brand new patient whom she describes as handsome, rich, and annoying.

Most people come here still struggling to accept that their life has changed in ways they will never come back from but apparently, this guy is taking it to a whole new level. She says he's refusing to learn any wheelchair skills and is completely fixated on walking out of here healed. It can happen. It's not likely but it can happen. I say a silent little prayer to G-d in my head that this man finds peace either way.

Get It On Amazon Now Or Wherever Books Are Sold!